Sex Game

A Game of Curiosity

Marcus Blake

Sex Game : *A Game of Curiosity*

A Starving Writers Book

Published by arrangement with the author

Copyright © 2007, 2008 by Starving Writers Publishing. Cover design by Starving Writers Publishing - All rights reserved. This book, or parts thereof, may not be reproduced in any form without permission.

The story is fictional and any resemblance to actual people, places, and certain facts is purely coincidence.

Starving Writers Publishing : Dallas Texas

www.starvingwriters.net

ISBN : 978-1-932996-16-6

Printed in the United States of America

Published in Dallas, Texas

For More information on Marcus Blake go to

www.marcusblake.net

www.myspace.com/themarcusblake

www.yoursexgame.org

~ About the Author ~

Marcus Blake was born in Chicago, Illinois in 1977. He grew up in Chicago and East Texas. His education is in History, Literature, Psychology, and Religion & Philosophy. Marcus Blake has studied at many universities throughout the United States, but his Alma Mata is Stephen F. Austin State University in Nacogdoches, Texas, which is also, where he wrote his first book, *The Music of Life*. Mr. Blake is a poet, writer, historian, and teacher. He has taught in the public school system, served in the Army, and has been a guest speaker at Education and Literary events throughout the world. Marcus Blake is now a full time writer, teacher, and lecturer. He makes his home in the Dallas Texas.

Other Books by Marcus Blake...

The Music of Life

My Reflections

Returning Home

Dedicated to the people in my life

that keep me curious everyday

Table of Contents

1. *The Beginning* — Pg. 9
2. *Jack and Sara* — Pg. 17
3. *Paula and Debbie* — Pg. 67
4. *Jen, Jarrod, and Sam* — Pg. 97
5. *Richard, Mike, and Nicole* — Pg. 137
6. *When All Hell Breaks Loose* — Pg. 197
7. *The Choices We Make* — Pg. 253
8. *The Ending We Choose to Make* — Pg. 299

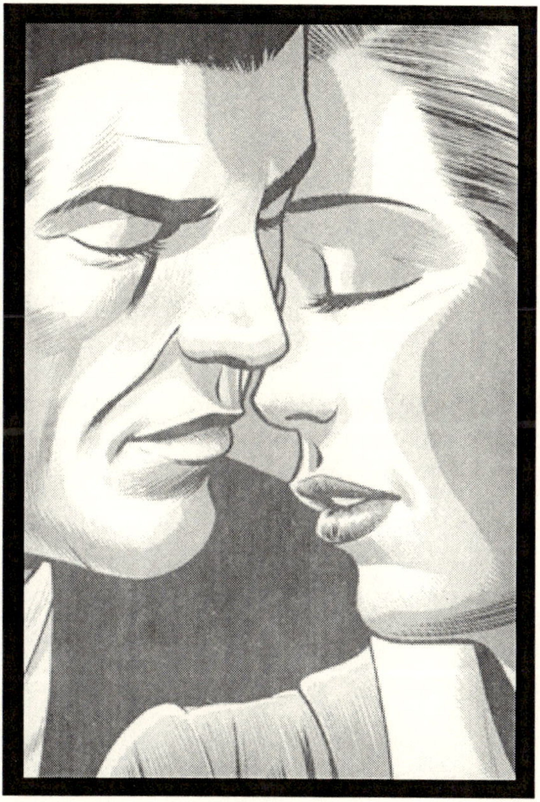

"Love does not begin and end the way we seem to think it does. Love is a battle, love is a war; love is a growing up."

"Love takes off masks that we fear we cannot live without and know we cannot live within."

~ James Baldwin

1

The Beginning

  Love, what do we really know about it? Is there anybody who has a clear-cut answer about what love truly is? Can anybody really break it down and define all of its ironies and complexities? Honestly, I don't think anybody has a real answer especially an old Spanish man like me that's been married for over forty years and to the same woman. I have to point out that I have been married to the same woman because it's a rarity that people stay married to one person for a long period of time. It also brings into question whether people have any idea of what love really is or what it takes to make it work.

Allow me to introduce myself since I am the one telling this sad but truthful story, my name is Trinidad and I own a bar called The Matador in downtown Chicago. It's not too far from the University of Chicago so I get a mixture of young patrons and working class stiffs from the surrounding neighborhoods that need a place with good beer and whiskey to blow off a little steam.

I meet all kinds of people and hear all kinds of stories. Most of the stories I hear are about important tragedies such as death, being swindled out of fortunes, and the ever so popular love and heartache. There are never a shortage of stories of how someone fell in love and then had their heart broken, but what I find pretty much every time is someone who was never really in love to begin with and if they were they didn't know how to fight for it.

Now don't get me wrong if there weren't people with these kind of stories then I wouldn't have people sitting at my bar whining about their lives and drinking my alcohol therefore putting money in my pocket. Happiness around here doesn't pay the bills, but I never get to tell a story where everything worked out for the best in the end. I certainly never have had any happy stories until this one that I can pass on to people who might need to hear them. However, just when you think there is never anything good you can tell people especially in the form of a great story one comes along for you to pass on.

There are a lot of regulars that come in and out of The Matador, some of which have been coming here since they were in college and some of them are friends of mine. There is one particular story of some of my young friends that I finally get to tell and its one of those interesting, joyful stories, which are far, and few. The story is sappy, romantic, tragic, crazy, and comical, but important because if nothing else searching for true love shouldn't be as hard as the characters of this story made it.

This story is universal because we have all lived it to some degree and we can all take a lesson from it. I know that I really can't give great advice when it comes to love compared to this story. Like I said before I've been married to the same woman for a very long time and I don't have much to go on. I could have cheated on her and had a great tale about the dark side of experience, but I'm married to a very feisty woman who would kill me in my sleep for committing that mortal sin and then cut my balls off just to be sure I was punished properly. Maybe Oscar Wilde was right, experience is the one thing you can't get for nothing. The other truth is I do love her, what can I say.

    The hard truth is, there is only one thing I know about love and it's something that I learned from the story of my young friends, love is just a sex game. Love is a sex game where we try to score at each other's expense and the rules we play by are worse than politics. It's a game where we most often mistake our sexual excursions for intimacy and blend our raw animal desires for true loving passion. You can look at it another way too, it's a game of curiosity where the players are filled with such duality that that we never know who they truly are. The players are just nameless faces waiting until they meet their tragic end within the realm of the broken hearted.

    We play the game time and time again and when we're bored, we change partners or if we don't like the rules, we change partners even though the rules are there to help us a long. The curiosity of the sex game is what keeps us playing and even though sometimes it resembles something like a cat; it's a drug that we just have to have no matter what the cost.

If we're lucky though, the sex game with all of its curiosity is one where we can find that permanent partner that keeps us playing till the end of our days while making life interesting and humbling all at the same time. Although something like that doesn't come along very often. The story I get to tell you is about playing that game of curiosity and doing the dance for the battle of our souls. It's a game we shouldn't have to lose, but losing is often done on our own accord. Although I am only a spectator the players are my friends Jack, Sarah, Richard, Paula, Mike, Nicole, Jen, Jarrod, Debbie, and the one I don't like, an asshole named Sam. Every great story has to have one. This is a great story and it's their story.

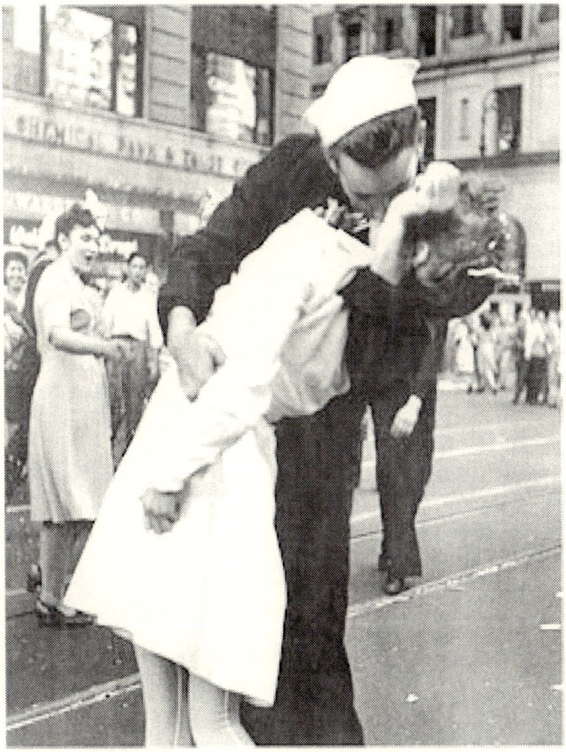

2

Jack and Sara

The Chicago north side apartment echoed with the sounds of packing. Luggage was being thrown around like nothing mattered. As Sara threw her cloths into her suitcases it added another layer to the stifling tension that her and Jack had created between them. Jack, her husband of ten years just stood there in the doorway of their bedroom drinking coffee and not braving the horrid sea of animosity Sara had for him now. Finally, he decided to say something and appeal to her rationale as if there really was any among the anger Sara had for the whole situation.

"Come on you don't actually have to pack and leave for good," Jack said.

Sara gave him a dirty look and replied back to him. "You really don't get it do you, I mean there is no getting through to you."

"What are talking about?"

"I told you last night that if we couldn't talk to each and be honest about our marriage I was leaving and this marriage would be over."

"I heard what you said last night and I was honest with you."

"No you decided to crack jokes and let your sarcasm do the talking even when I asked you not to."

"You asked me if we had a chance at making it what percent it would be and I answered your question."

"You said ten percent."

"Yeah, my honest answer it ten percent; we have a ten percent chance of making this work."

"If that's true then we have a ninety percent chance of not making it, so what the hell is the point." Sara said to Jack in an angry tone as she pushed Jack out of the way so she could get things out of the bathroom.

Jack shook his head at her and said. "No, that's not what it means. You're looking at this all wrong. You have to take ten percent off for every year of marriage so in actuality ten percent is really like a hundred percent. So we really have a hundred percent of working out."

Sara paused for a moment with a surprised look on her face. Then she said to Jack. "That's the stupidest thing I've ever heard, it doesn't even make sense."

"Sure it does, it's all about semantics and different parts of a marriage have to be measured differently because once you get past the first few years which are the most turbulent then it gets easier and you can start reducing the percent level of success or failure." Jack said to Sara in his confident tone.

"You see now you're just making that up. There is no such thing as different degrees in marriage; it's all the same whether you're married 1 year, 10 years, or 40 years."

"No it isn't. There are semantics to how this really works because if you can make it ten years in marriage then the hard part is over. It's all downhill from there."

Sara looked him with her very serious, angry look, it was the look that let people around her know that the gates of hell were about to be opened and her fury would be let out. She said to Jack. "You know where you can put your semantics..."

Jack cut her off before she could finish her sentence and replied. "Hey there missy, there's no need to get nasty."

Sara picked up her cup of coffee and threw it at Jack. She hated when he called her missy even when he was joking around. It wasn't because of the sexist overtone as one might think, as it turned out Jack had an ex girlfriend named missy and she was the one before Sara came into his life. Calling her missy was not the way to appeal to Sara's compassion or rationale; in fact, it was the biggest no, no of them all when it came to Sara even more so than calling her a bitch, a whore, or a cunt. Jack knew this, but sometimes he would do it just make her mad. It was his way of holding his own in the marriage, not necessarily a happy one, and that was part of the reason why.

Jack had ducked in time before the coffee cup hit him in the head. Sara had a great arm, she had played college softball and even though she had not played for ten years she was just as good now as she was then. Jack had always feared that he would make her so mad that one day just like an outfielder trying to get the runner out at home she would nail him with something from across the room. He never stopped testing that theory, no matter how stupid comment was, Yet it was another reason their marriage might not be as good as it should have been after ten years.

    They didn't say anything to each other after Sara threw her coffee cup at Jack. There was nothing to say, their marriage had always been rocky at best and this particular morning was the straw that broke the camel's back. All Sara did was finish packing and walk out the door. Jack didn't do anything to try and stop her, he didn't know how. She had left before when she was angry, but it had always been for a day so she could clear her head and calm down. She had never left with her belongings as if she was moving away. This time however, she was finally calling it quits; as far as she was concerned the marriage was over.

    Jack stood at their living room that over looked the streets below and watched her load her suitcases into a taxi then watched ad it drove away. He didn't know what say to her and what he could have done to stop her this time. Whether it was out of pride or stubbornness, or he just plain didn't know how Jack didn't ever try to stop Sara. All he could do was stand at the window watching the L-train go roaring by with the attitude of shock and surprise.

After he stood at the window for about twenty minutes watching the streets below hoping that she would come back he finally gave up on that notion. He did what he always did when he needed to talk and get it all in the open. He called his brother. It was 7am and even though he knew that his brother would still be in bed because his job as a journalist kept him working late into the night Jack called him anyway.

The phone let out a series of annoying rings at Richard's place. It took him a few moments to collect his thoughts as his cell phone rang, but finally he leaned over to his nightstand and looked at the caller ID to see who was calling. He saw that it was his brother Jack so he picked up the phone and answered. "What could you possibly want at 7am that you had to wake me up?"

Jack let out a laugh and said to his brother. "You know normal people are usually up at 7am getting ready for work, not lounging around in bed."

"Normal people have 9 to 5 jobs; mine keeps me working very late to which I did not get to bed until a few hours ago."

"What was her name that kept you up that late?"

"I wish I was that lucky."

"Get up and get dressed, I need to talk to you."

"Can't you talk to me later when there is a happy hour somewhere?"

"Its important, it's about Sara."

"Look I love you, Bro, but its way too early to listen to you complain about you wife, that's for when I'm not sober."

"She left me this morning and she actually packed her bag so I know she's not coming back."

"Oh, so its one of those conversations!"

"Yeah it's going to be ones of those conversations."

"Alright, I'll get dressed and meet you at the diner, but you're buying me breakfast."

"Fine, but I might actually need your help this time."

With that said, Jack hung up the phone and left. Richard slowly got himself out of bed desperately trying to find where he put his pants with his wallet and keys still in them. Getting phone calls like that was not unusual, his family was very big on talking out their feelings and the best people to do that with was always family. Although sometimes it was not that fun, it was family and no matter what you had to be there for them even through the stupid conversations. Sometimes you just have to talk out your love problems in order to make sense out of everything.

The diner they usually met at was a few streets over where from where both Jack and Richard lived. It was in walking distance, but was one of those places that was always more convenient by way of the L-train. Since it was early in the morning and people would be on their way to work Jack and Richard both walked to the diner that morning. For Richard it was not that great of walk, but walking is not that fun with a hangover and his body let him know about it. When Richard finally arrived at the diner, he found his brother Jack sitting in the corner with a cup a coffee.

Richard walked up to his brother sat down at the table and replied. "It's not nice to make someone walk this far with a hangover."

Jack gave him a sarcastic look and said. "You shouldn't party like that anymore; you're getting too old for it. We can't drink like we're nineteen again."

"You mean like how you got through law school."

"You see God will just keep punishing you today for making comments like that especially when I'm all broken hearted and I need someone to console me."

"Yeah, you look it, by the way why do you always call me to talk this early in the morning. We have a sister you can call and you know she'll be honest with you."

"True, but every time I call Jen, her boyfriend Sam answers and I get to hear him say in his dumbass redneck voice," Jack did the impersonation, "damn it who the fuck is calling, is there no decency."

They both started laughing because Jack did an almost perfect impersonation of Sam who did talk like a redneck and talking with him caused your IQ to be lowered. Finally, Richard continued with the conversation.

"So she really left you this morning, do you think it's for good?"

Jack sighed for a moment and replied to his brother. "I think so, she did pack her bags and you don't pack that much stuff just to leave for a few days."

"Well she's left before and sometimes she just stayed a night with one of her friends. She's even stayed without sister a few times because she did not want to be in the same house with you. What makes you think that this time will be any different?"

"She said she was leaving the marriage if we couldn't talk or be honest with each other."

"Did you guys talk about it, were you honest with her?"

"Of course we talked about it and yes I was honest with her."

"What did she ask you? I know she asked you something and you screwed up the answer didn't you?"

"No, she asked me last night what chance I thought we had of making it and I answered her honestly."

Richard gave his brother a disgruntled looked and started shaking his head no. He then replied to Jack. "I can't believe it; you gave her the semantic argument about your marriage."

"So what if I did, I wasn't wrong. She asked what percent we had and I said ten percent and then explained the different degrees of marriage based on the years you've been married."

"Look I know that with that kind of logic you are not wrong, but women don't see it that way therefore you can't use the semantic argument with them about your marriage."

"I explained how it works to her so she would understand, she's a smart woman she should see it how it works."

"Jack you are the dumbest smart person I know. Semantics get thrown right out the door with women. They don't mean anything because they don't think in logical terms like we do."

"How come you know so much about women and marriage when you've never been married?"

"Hey, I'm not stupid. Besides, at least I've never gotten married and then screwed it up. There is only one person at this table that's done that."

Jack paused for a moment and gave his brother a dirty look. He knew he was right, but you never concede that point within sibling rivalry. Finally, he said to Richard. "I may not have screwed it up yet; she could calm down today and come home."

"Do you really think that?" Richard asked his brother sarcastically. "I mean you might even get that three-way you've always wanted, but do you think it's really going to happen?"

"You know I wanted to talk to you so I could feel better about myself since I had a beautiful woman that loved me and you're still searching for the right one out of all the crazy women you date. You're my brother aren't you supposed to make me feel better?"

"It's too early for whisky so I can't do that and just for your information I've never been credited with screwing up a relationship because I couldn't be honest with someone. Besides it's never your fault when the women you date are like a walking pharmacy filled with anti-psychotic drugs... its just bad karma.

"Yeah I do think God's punishing you for something."

Richard gave a sarcastic smile to Jack while the waitress came over to take their breakfast order. After a refill on their coffee, they continued their conversation. Jack spoke up and said. "I can't believe this is really happening, I never thought it would end especially when getting over what happened five years ago."

"You mean when you guys cheated on each other. If a marriage was going to end over something then infidelity would be it, but you did get through it so maybe you can get through this."

"True, but maybe we never really did. Maybe she still hates me and maybe I don't really want to be married anymore. Maybe we never called it quits because we didn't want to find a new place to live because being with each other was comfortable."

Richard gave Jack a very serious look and then asked him. "Be honest, do you really want to be married to Sara anymore because maybe you're right, you only stay with her because you're comfortable."

Jack thought for a moment and replied. "I don't know. I don't mind that she's there, but I don't mind when she's not there."

"Congratulations, you just described mom and dad so it's not really an answer. Let me ask you this, when she's gone do you miss her?"

Jack thought again and he answered. "Sometimes I do, but not like I use to then again there are moments when I need her to be there even if it's just being in the same room."

Richard laughed and replied back. "Then my friend you're royally screwed. If you can't figure out what you really want then you will never how to get it."

"I can't believe I'm getting wisdom from a man who still likes to sleep around with young grad students and whose last date ended with her leading police in a high speed chase when they tried to pull her over for speeding."

"Hey I'm not saying that my love life isn't adventurous, but I also know what I am looking for when it comes to having a serious relationship. Most of the time I just fool around to keep from being bored."

"I have to admit my relationship problems are not that bad compared to yours. The thing is though, I usually have the answer and I don't have it now, I honestly don't know what to do."

Richard looked at his brother with regret and said to him. "I can't tell you what to do except, you have to figure out if you really want to be married to her anymore. If you have a hard time trying to figure it out treat it like a court case. Break it down, go back to the beginning, and piece everything together so you can figure it out. That's how you think anyway."

Jack thought for moment and gave out a small laugh. Then he replied. "I may need a lot of legal pads for this one."

"Maybe, but you're being forced to go back and figure out how you really got here so you can find out what you really want. That's going to be the hard part."

With that said Richard ate his breakfast in a hurry and then left so he could get to work. Jack did the same. He wanted to get home early that night because he had a lot to think about; he had many things to remember.

Jack got home early that day and he went about his usual business, he didn't even wait around for Sara to come home. He knew that she probably wouldn't be coming home so for the first time in ten years he made dinner for one and prepared to be alone. Jack didn't know what to do because it seemed that he was starting to get on with his life by himself. When Sara would leave for a night, he would just grab take out so he wouldn't have to make a dinner for just one person. This time it was different, it was the end of his marriage and the beginning of how to live again on his own.

After dinner, he sat down with a nice glass of brandy and started to think back before he met Sara, trying to get a feel for what life was like before her and then trying to remember how they met. Jack met Sara in college when they were both students at the University of Chicago. It was in there sophomore year as they both turned twenty years of age finally entering into true adult years and breaking the chains of their teens. Jack was pre-law and at the time, Sara was pre-med but she figured out early in her sophomore year that she was not cut out for medicine and that the site of blood made her queasy.

    Jack on the other hand was well suited for the law because his thought process was based on a level of degrees and theory. For Jack it was a good thing and bad thing, good for the law and the courtroom, but bad in dealing with people. Sometime towards the end of the winter semester, Jack and Sara met each other in the library by accident as they tried to check out the same book. It just so happened that they both had the same history class and needed the same book for a research paper. They both argued over who was going to check out the book until they were kicked out of the library for being too loud. Also both of them didn't get to check out the book, at least that's how Jack remembered it.

Somewhere in between all the arguing Jack and Sara found they both had something in common; they both liked to argue and they had to be right all the time. So when it came time to finish the research for their papers they helped each other out by doing the research together. It was more of a help for Sara since she was not a true history person and not very good at writing historical papers. Jack was a history enthusiast; he loved history and loved to talk about it. He would talk about it with anybody he could even if they didn't want to talk History with him. Writing long winded boring papers as Sara used call to call them just came natural for Jack and he could even get a novas to write a great paper. That's what he did for Sara the first time they ever spent any time together.

Despite their constant arguing there was something there and they began to challenge each other, as lovers should do to keep things alive. From that time on, they spent most of their free time together, dating and then eventually becoming serious. A few months turned into a year for them and a year turned into three until they graduated college. Jack graduated with a general studies degree on his way to Law School at the University of Chicago and Sara with a marketing degree, she found she was a better salesmen than somebody who should be in medicine.

By the time college had ended they had done all the usual things a couple does, they had met each other's family, they had spent holidays together, and they even started living together their last year making each other truly serious about their future together. So as it happened after graduation Jack had gotten his acceptance to law school at the University of Chicago and Sarah started working on her MBA they were out one night having dinner at one of their favorite places to eat and they started to talk about the future. They both knew that they would have to talk about it eventually and make their plans with or without each other.

Jack was the one to bring it up first; Sara wanted to, but she was smart enough to know that Jack wasn't the type to be rushed in life. He like to just go along and let life happen, it would be a good thing and a bad thing for him. As they were eating dinner Jack started the conversation He didn't exactly know what he would say, but he started talking about it with Sara anyway.

"So do you have any big plans for the rest of your life besides finishing your education?" Jack asked Sara with a peculiar look on his face.

"Are you asking me what I have planned in my career or my personal life?"

"I guess I'm referring to your personal life, I mean do you see yourself married someday."

"Only since I was seven years old playing house with my sisters. Why are you asking?"

"Well its something we've never talked about and you always say we should find new things to talk about."

Sara started laughing; she was a little excited that Jack had finally gotten around to talking about marriage. She knew that Jack was not the big romantic type; he was more like the small gestures once in a while type of guy. This kind of conversation was hard for Jack so it took him a little bit longer to get to the point even if it was time to have it since they had been dating for three years now.

Sara finally replied back to Jack. "If there's something on your mind that you want to talk about then come out and say it. We've been with each other for too long to keep side-stepping the issue and we don't have to fake it."

"Sara do you love me. I mean really love me?"

"Yes I do, but you have your moments that really make me what to forget about you. Do you love me?"

Jack paused for a moment as if he was going to give her devastating news. Sara looked at him with a worried look thinking that he was going to break up with her and that he was a real bastard for doing it in a public place so she wouldn't make a scene. She said to herself in that she was not going to give him that courtesy if he really broke up with her in the restaurant. Finally, he surprised her, not with a ring because he wasn't the type to buy one with the chance of her saying no.

Jack looked at her with a serious look and said. "Sara I do love you... do you want to get married?"

"She looked with a sarcastic look and replied. "You're not even going to get down on one knee."

He had a surprised look on his face when she said that and then he realized that he was not being very romantic. He got up from his seat and got down on one knee asking her again. "Do you want to get married?"

Sara laughed and said as she leaned to whisper in his ear. "I was only kidding about the knee thing. You know you don't have to be that traditional with me, but it nice of you to make the effort, that's what really counts."

Jack got off his knee and sat back down then looked at her with an impatient look waiting to hear an answer. After a brief a pause he finally asked Sara. "Well do you have answer?"

"No, but I have a question, do you really want to get married to me or are you doing this because you think you have to ask because it's the next step and you're afraid of losing me."

"I don't want to lose you and yes I figured this was the next step so I thought I would ask and she what you'd said."

"Do you want to keep dating me or do you really want to be married because if you don't then we don't have to."

"I love you Sara and I don't want to be with anybody else. I can't see myself with anybody else for the rest of my life."

"I'm flattered and I don't want to be with anybody else; I've known that for the last three years, but you still haven't answered my question, do you really want to be married?"

"Well you never answered my question about being married."

"You pretty much know what my answer will be after I just said I don't want to be with anybody else, but can you answer the question?"

Jack just looked at her speechless because he knew that he was avoiding the real question. Sara was calling him on it and she was one of the few people that could actually call him out when he was avoiding a question or arguing over semantics. This was one of the things that he loved about her and it was hard to get mad at her. Sometimes he would force her to get angry so he could easily beat her in an argument and continue not answering the real question.

After a few moments of not talking Sara suggested something daring to help the both of them be completely honest in answering the question. She said to Jack. "Why don't we do this, let's each take a cocktail napkin sign out names to them with our answer of yes or no."

Jack agreed and they each grabbed a cocktail napkin that was sitting off to the side of their table and put their answers on them above their signature. They didn't show each other for a moment and finally Sara said. "Okay, I'll show you mine if you show me yours."

"Okay," said Jack.

"The both held up their napkins to each other and they both had a look of joy as they looked at the other's napkin. Both cocktail napkins said yes and then Sara suggested that they exchange napkins and keep the other's answer as a reminder of what their answers were. They leaned across the table and kissed.

    Neither of them were that excited about a big wedding and it wasn't like they didn't think of each other as being married anyway. Originally, they planned a small ceremony, but before everything was set in stone one afternoon they just went to city hall, found a judge and got married. Later their families did throw them a big party giving them lots of gifts and money so they both could finish school. That's what Jack and Sara did, they were married on a whim, struggled to finish law school and an MBA working small jobs just to make it. Overall, it was the best years of their marriage Jack recalled. It was these thoughts that he held close for the next few days; he honestly didn't know what to completely feel when it came to Sara leaving. All he did know was that he missed her.

    Jack and Sara did not speak to each other for about ten days. They didn't even try to contact each other. Jack knew that she would call when she had time to think and her anger wasn't in control of her thoughts. Finally, she did call and asked to meet him so they could discuss what to do next. It was a Thursday night and they met at familiar place, The Matador, a place that they had been going to since college. It had a lot of memories for them, as Sara pointed out they needed familiarity in order to get through the conversations they were about to have.

They met and found a booth in the back that was out of the way from people and their usual drunken conversations. The cocktail waitress brought them a couple of drinks as they made small talk about work to avoid the real subject. Finally, Jack asked her where she was staying. She responded that she was staying at her sister's place. Before he could ask any more questions, she stopped him so she could talk and be really honest as she called it.

Sara said to Jack. "I need you to be quiet for a moment and let me talk so I could get this out. No interruptions."

"Okay, what do you need to say." Jack replied in a somber tone.

"I've had time to think and I don't want to keep doing this anymore because it seems like we keep going round and round doing the same dance until nothing gets solved."

"What do you want to do, get a divorce?" Jack asked her in a saddened tone.

"Yes, I do. I think it's for the best and we both know that we can't do counseling at this point. We're never going to do it 100%."

"I can do counseling if that's what you really want."

"Know you can't and I can't either. If we couldn't do it five years ago when we really should have done it then we're certainly not going to do it now. If we are going to get past this then we need a clean break."

"Then let's separate for little while or go on a trip strapping ourselves in chair forcing ourselves deal with our problems until their solved."

"An old law school trick where your forced to figure out a problem before you can leave is not going to work. All we'll do is get mad at each other and then end up doing something that we'll both regret."

"Okay, I don't want to do anything you don't want to do. If a divorce is what you really want then we will do it. I guess we should talk about the apartment and out belongings."

Sara smiled at him, she smiled at the practical lawyer in him for he was always ready to get down to business and never waist time. It was something that was not in his nature. It was also part of what made her fall in love with him. She paused and smiled then took one of his hands to let him know that it would be okay.

Sara replied Jack. "I think we should make this easy. I don't want the apartment so you can have it. I don't care about the furniture because I can get more. Our savings we can split down the middle. You have your retirement, your income, your car, and I have mine. We just change all of our insurance and we go our separate ways."

Jack smiled at her and said. "Then I will file for divorce tomorrow and we'll do it under irreconcilable differences."

"That's good and we don't have to have messy fight for anything because to be honest I'm okay with walking away completely just to avoid a messy fight."

That was it, no argument, no petitioning for anything, no protests and no solemn remarks. Jack and Sara were done just like that. They finished their drinks engaged in some more small talk even laughing a little bit. It was the most fun they had had in long time and one would have never known that they were getting a divorce After a while Sara left leaving Jack there to drink alone. While he was there, he had one drink after another running up a pretty lengthy bar tab.

Two hours after Sara left and he was really drunk he started to get loud and get belligerent spouting off all sorts of nuances about the law for those that would listen even to some that would not. He was in no shape to drive home and definitely in no shape to get home on his own so I did what he always did when one of the Anderson kids got carried away. His brother was called. I actually had his and Jack's number as an emergency number just in case since they were regulars.

As Jack was half way passed out in his booth dead drunk Richard showed up to collect his brother. He entered the bar and said. "I guess my brother was his usual charming self tonight."

I replied. "You can say that, He was here with Sara and after she left that's when he got really drunk."

"That'll definitely do it."

"Tonight he decided teach the other patrons about the law and philosophy."

"Wow he must be really drunk, here's my card to take care of his bill."

I grabbed the credit card and took care of the bill while smiling in amusement at Richard's comments. Richard was the funny one and spared no expense to throw out sarcasm. Richard walked over to the booth that contained his drunk brother and he replied. "Well, I see you're having a fun night."

"Hey man, why didn't you tell me that you were coming by, I would have gotten you a drink before you arrived or six or seven drinks."

"You mean so I can catch up with you. You're a thoughtful brother. I don't know what I would do without you?"

"I'm glad you got here because I've been talking with all these great people and they've really been listening."

"Jack have you been teaching the law while you've been drinking; I thought we had talked about that. You know you're not supposed to be doing that because you start acting like a bigger than normal jerk."

"I'm sorry...I'm sorry man, but I love you brother."

"I know you do."

Jack paused for a moment and leaned back in the booth while getting a little emotional. He was trying to hide the tears he was starting to let out. Richard asked his brother. "Hey, what's wrong, why are you starting to cry?"

"It's over...Sara told me tonight that she wanted a divorce."

"You kind of knew that it was coming after she left this time. It's been coming for a long time now, right."

"She didn't even want to work it out; she just wanted to give up on us."

"I think she's figured out that if you two are going to have any kind of chance of being happy you're going have to make a clean break and maybe it's time that you do. Maybe it's time that you just want different things now in your life and what you thought you once had isn't going to last a life time. It happens Jack... it's a part of life."

"I know, I just never thought it would happen to me."

"Who really expects it to happen to them?"

Jack shrugged his shoulders and said. "I've never been dumped before; I always did the dumping so it's a little different for me now."

"So what it's really about is you being dumped by Sara, Would it have made it easier if you asked her for the divorce?"

"I don't know, maybe not."

"That's the one thing you've said tonight that's made sense."

"I just can't believe it's finally over. Now I've got to learn to do things for myself again."

"You'll be alright; it will come back to you."

"What if it doesn't?"

"Shit man, you're a lawyer with a 180 IQ, I think you can learn it again."

"Maybe all I can do is struggle through life never doing anything for myself until eventually I die because I couldn't do anything for myself."

Richard got up and helped Jack to his feet so he could get him home. He then replied to his brother. "Look brother let's just get you home, you're drunken philosophy is not impressing me."

"I don't want to go home yet, I need to talk to Sara."

"No, that's the one thing you definitely don't need to do. Let me get you home and into bed. We'll play the Ben Folds Five song-A Song for the Dumped, you can call Sara a bitch, and then you'll be alright in the morning."

"You're a good brother, why are you doing this for me anyway."

"Someday I might wanted for murder and I'm going to need a good lawyer to help me out for free and when that day comes you don't get to ask any questions of why. Besides you are my brother who else would be doing this for you."

Richard helped Jack out of the bar, waved to me and I couldn't help but laugh. He got Jack home and dropped him in his bed taking his shoes off so he could sleep somewhat comfortable even though he would be sleeping in his whiskey-scented cloths. Richard set the coffee maker on "timer" matching the alarm clock in the bedroom. He knew that in the morning Jack was really going to need it.

∞∞∞∞∞

Over the next week or so, maybe it was more like two or three weeks Jack thought a lot more about the past. He had filed for divorce just as he said and everything went according to plan in dividing everything with Sara. They didn't fight and they were fairly nice to each other as they moved her out of the apartment while also dividing their assets with one another. The conversations they had while doing all of that were the best conversations they had, had in years, which was pretty pathetic considering they were getting a divorce.

Jack's thoughts about the past were mainly about him and Sara, everything from when they were first married to how they got to this point in their lives. He didn't spend much time working at the office; he just stared most of the time at the pictures in his office. He didn't want to take the pictures of Sara down yet, for some reason it just felt wrong. All he could do was spend most of his time looking at the pictures on the wall and remembering.

When Jack and Sara were first married, everything seemed perfect Jack recalled. It was as if they had first met each other and they were in that new exciting relationship where all they did was just be around each other even if they were not having sex. Jack and Sara had heard about couples that were together for a long time where everything was great when they were dating, bust as soon as they got married it all changed and the marriage didn't last a full year. For Jack and Sara it was not that way. Marriage actually made their relationship stronger as funny as it might sound.

They didn't have much money or a lot of things back then, no big screen TVs or really nice furniture, they didn't even have internet access or cable TV because they couldn't afford it. No matter what they made it and their everyday lives were great, just like that *leave it to beaver* bullshit that everybody believes is a façade. However for Jack and Sara it was true because all they had was each other and it was enough.

Their lives were busy with grad school and law school. For Jack it was very time consuming and with all the studying Jack's days were like a twenty hour work days, but no matter what he always made time for Sara even if it was three in the morning when they both had to be up at five. When they were not wrapped up in school activities they would have their fun. Their fun was what Jack and Sara called *No Money* Fun. Whatever they did had to cost nothing, but still be entertaining.

They would do things like walk around the heart of Chicago; places like State and Clark and Lake Michigan watching the people in a hurry with their everyday lives while they would take it slow trying not to grow up too fast. For concerts they would sit on the hill tops of

Grant Park and listen to the Chicago Symphony play during the summer time. Sometimes for meals all they would have is a pop and a traditional Chicago Hot dog with everything on it from one of the many local street vendors. In addition, if they were really big spenders they would hop a bus to Milwaukee and get whatever baseball tickets were left over only a dollar in cost for the Cubs and Brewers. It wasn't Wrigley Field, but it was like vacation that only cost twenty dollars.

For some odd reason, Jack thought, it was the best times of their lives before careers and routine got in the way; before some sense of normal working lives got in the way. For the first two years of marriage despite the long hours of school and studying they were there for each other and never let a thing like neglect get in the way. They never let what was going on in their lives interrupt what was going on in their relationship. In fact for those first two years the only thing they had to fight was from having too much fun as crazy as it might sound. Boredom never got in the way and going through the motions was nonexistent.

Finally Jack and Sara graduated with their post grad degrees and took full time jobs, her at a PR firm in downtown

Chicago and Jack at a small law firm in downtown Chicago not too fare from where they lived now. That's when it started, all the things that never got in the way before were suddenly apart of their everyday lives and routine was a permanent visitor. They both started working long hours in their jobs trying to move up in their careers and the hard work paid off. Both of them would be promoted and start making lots of money. However, with all their successes Jack and Sara spent less and less time together and talked even less than those first two years.

Their hours in the day would be different so they didn't see other much except when they woke up together and shared the newspaper over morning coffee. Even then they didn't really talk, just got ready for another workday. Since they started having different hours eating dinner together became harder and harder. The first few years after they had started their careers the only time they really spent any significant time together was during holidays. Of course there was a week's vacation that they took during that five-year period, but one week's vacation in five years never really help anybody. For Jack and Sara all it became was a reminder that they were still married to one another.

After being married for five years they had finally become that typical couple; too consumed with careers and making money that they worked more than being in a marriage. They made their money, they became successful, and they even tried to fulfill some missing hole they had been created with buying each other expensive things. Each of them got a new car every year, they had that big screen TV, she has lots of expensive Jewelry, and he had his many toys that guys like to buy. They had everything but that one perfect moment that reminded each of them why they loved each other, why they would fight for each other. They never had any great conversation filled with laughter anymore. It seemed that the only good conversations they could have were with heated words and a disdained tone.

So finally it happened, the breaking point, the moment that makes it all come crashing down. Jack and Sara had grown apart and they spent more time being mad at each other, although both of them couldn't remember why anymore. Jack and Sara had not seen each other very much with the hours they were working and when they did see each other all they did was fight so they decided to take a break for while. They weren't separating exactly, just taking a break for a few weeks so they could see things more clearly. It was more like as mini vacation if you will. Sara moved out and went to live with one of her younger sisters.

    They would be away from each other for a month. They wouldn't call or email and they would continue their normal lives except without each other. They did just that and by the time the month was done they had a new perspective on things, but it's what they did during that time away from each other that would forever change their lives and make them see the whole god forsaken truth about being in a relationship.

    During the month apart Jack and Sara both continued to work long hours and live their normal lives, just without each other. At Jack's office, two things happened that would save and ruin his life to a certain point. The first thing was, an old friend of Sara's came to work at the law office, which meant there was nothing that could be kept a secret when it came to his actions. The second thing was, he would have an affair with somebody at the office.

It wasn't that Sara's friend Jackie was mean and deliberately told Sara everything that Jack did at work; it's that she just couldn't keep a secret and loved to gossip. The woman Jack would have an affair with was a young paralegal working there who was very pretty and loved to flirt. She was also nice to Jack, which was something that he had not had in a long time with Sara. The affair happened one night when they were working late and then people from the office went out to get a few drinks. It was innocent and Jack was not even drunk. He was lonely even though he didn't want to admit it so when she invited him back to her place he went. They had a wild and passionate night, something else that Jack had not had in a long time.

It only happened once and Jack could remember how guilty he felt about the whole thing. As far as he was concerned he would never do it again and just forget about it, but he wasn't that lucky. Secrets like office sex almost never remain a secret and Sara had a friend working at the office. Sara did find out about it and in her moments of anger and disdain for Jack decided to take it out on a night with her girlfriends. She figured the best way to ignore the phone calls by

Jack pleading for forgiveness and get past the anger was to have a wild night with her girlfriends hitting all the cool spots in Chicago with a bottle of Tequila as her co-pilot.

What Sara found out was that revenge never happens the way one thinks it does. Somehow guilt and stupidity were mixed with it. In her drunken night of fun she found a guy to go home with and ended up doing the same thing Jack did to her. Did it make her feel better, no? Does something like that ever make anybody feel better, what do you think? Of course karma had a strange sense of humor with her as well; her friend Jackie was out with them that night. Jack would find out about it, not necessarily from Jackie, although that happened as well, but the guy Sara was with turned out to be a client and we all know how guys like to talk.

One month turned into three months for the separation of Jack and Sara. Finally they met each other at The Matador, the place of good times and bad news. The met each other to talk about the future. They almost got a divorce then and there, but whatever fight they had for each other came out at the right moment. Jack could recall the conversation he had with Sara that night while they just kept getting served drinks hoping to relax and to get all their crazy notions out into the open.

Jack asked Sara that night while sitting in a booth in the back corner of the bar. "Okay so we've both managed to hurt each other and get back at one another, where do we go from here?"

"I guess that depends on you," she replied in a serious tone.

"Do you want a divorce; If you do you'll have a fight on your hands without a leg to stand on since we're both to blame for all of this."Jack said to her.

"You know that's just like you, you always have to puff up your chest and show everybody whose man while putting the blame on someone else."

"What, I'm not trying to get into a fight with you about this. I'm just merely pointing out that if we get a divorce we can't really blame the other person since we're both at fault."

"Jack, I'm not stupid, don't treat me like I am. I never said everything was your fault."

"Okay, noted. Now what do you want to do?"

"Do you still want to be married to me?"
"Do you still want to be married to me?"

"I asked you first."

"Well as funny as it might sound... yeah I do." Jack said to Sara.

"Okay then. I still want to be married to you as well, but our lives have to change or we're going to end up here again."

"You're right I think we did what we did just to hurt each other."

"Maybe or maybe not, but we can't keep doing it the way we've been doing it. Somehow we lost was we had those first two years and we need to it back."

"I agree, everything seemed simpler and better back then."

"It was. Now what do we do to get it back."

Jack and Sara both realized that they had let their careers and everyday lives get in the way so all that they knew was routine. That night they talked about what was missing in their relationship. They made their plans to get it back and be what they really wanted to be. Sara moved back in and they took a two-week vacation something they had never done. They went to places that they had always talked about going to, but could never afford until now. It was a good thing for them and as a couple they became great again.

They did things together again and they did things as couple should do together like go to movies and go out to dinner with other couples. Some of the things they did were therapeutic couple's activities used to strength their relationship. Sara even got Jack to take a ballroom dancing class with her and they learned how to swing, salsa, and even tango. It wasn't really that much fun for Jack, but he was with Sara gain and that made the difference. For the next year after that everything was great and they settled back into their old selves again just like they were when they first got married. They even stayed up talking in bed and spent Sunday mornings together reading the newspaper, watching old movies, and napping with each other.

For a while everything was good again, but it wouldn't last. Eventually they settled back into their old routines of working long hours and eating dinner alone. They didn't fight as much, they just didn't talk with each other and when they did have a conversation it didn't even seem real, just the shadow of existing words. They used to talk about having kids now they didn't do that anymore and the holidays would come and go where it would be the only time they really spent any quality time together.

For a while they didn't even notice what had happened to each other. When they were in bed together they were miles and sometimes worlds away from each other. The foot between them became a lifetime away from each other compared to when they used to be in a room together yards away at opposite ends of the room a but it seemed like they were only inches from one another. So finally after another five years had gone by they had ended up where they had been once before. It had nothing to do with being in their thirties and life not being what they had expected after turning thirty. They had been in slow monotonous steps until they arrived right back to the shitty part of being married.

They were thirty-three, no kids, more money than they had every planed on making in their lifetime and their life together had become going through the motions. They never even peaked from behind the masks they had created for each other. So one night Sara finally asked Jack the question, the question about what chance he thought they had of making it. After he made a sarcastic remark she finally told him that it was no used being married if they couldn't talk to each other or just be honest with each other. The next day she packed and left for good.

Six months after that day Jack and Sara's divorce was finalized and they were officially single again. They had a nice quiet drink at The Matador to go over the final paper work and settlements, but really just to say goodbye. They had parted on good terms even to the point that they could actually talk to each other outside of being married to one another. As Jack gave her copies of everything he asked her. "Do you have any regrets about anything?"

Sara laughed and replied. "You want to do this now, now that we are finally divorced."

"This isn't some sad and pathetic way of strolling down memory lane with you. I was just curious."

"Sure, I have some regrets like working too much. Do you?"

"I regret not taking you on that cruise you wanted to go on three years ago."

"Really, I thought you were relieved we didn't go, after all you hate the water." Sara said while laughing a little bit.

"Yeah, but you wanted to go and I should have taken you."

"You don't think that would have solved all our problems do you?"

"No, I'm not that foolish, but I should've taken you on that cruise."

Sara thought for a moment and then replied. "I really wish that we would have talked more over the last few years just like we did ten years ago. I wish you would have been more honest with me instead of being sarcastic."

"I probably won't ever be like that. Maybe as I get older I'll spend less and less talking about my feelings just like my dad."

"Maybe, but it would be a shame."

Sara looked at him with a somber look and they paused for a moment not knowing what to say then she finally asked Jack. "Did you keep the napkin I gave you with my answer to your marriage proposal on it?"

Jack thought for moment because it had been a long time since he had thought about that. He answered. "I don't think so. I think it got lost among my things then again I may have thrown it away, why do you ask?"

"I was just curious. Well since we're done I got to go, Things to do and places to be."

"Already have a big date"

"No, I think you killed the dating scene for me, don't tell me you already have one."

"Hell no, I don't even know how to date anymore. I wouldn't know what to do. I got plans with Richard; he's got tickets for the Cubs tonight."

"Well there's nothing like beer and bratwurst to get over a divorce, I might have to see if my girlfriends want to do that."

They smiled at each other over their sarcasm. They both knew that, that kind of playful banter was going to be missed by the both of them. They hugged and told each other that they would see each other around and then Sara left. The truth was they didn't see each other for almost two years after that; it would be the most unusual of circumstances.

About two years later Jack arrived at his office early. Jackie was still working there and as strange as it might sound her and Jack had become good friends. She was still a friend to Sara and as a courtesy to the both Sara and Jack she would never tell them about each other.

Jack knew very little about what had happened to Sara since their divorce. His life was work now and he didn't even date. Sometimes he would go out with

Richard and his roommate Mike, but he never really pursued anything with a woman. Jack just assumed that Sara was going through a similar life or maybe that's just what he wanted to believe. He never knew because he never gave much thought about it. That is until he was walking past Jackie's desk one early morning and he saw a shocking object lying on her desk. He stared at it with disbelief for the longest time. It was a wedding invitation for Jackie. Sara was getting married again.

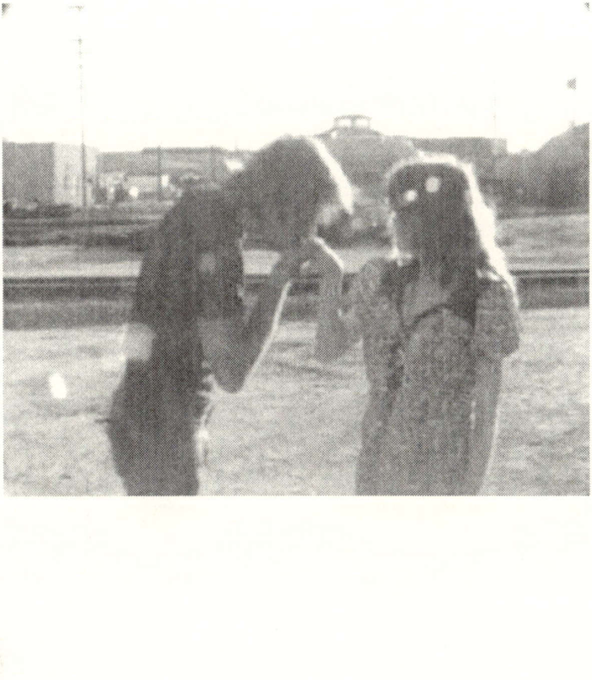

3

Paula and Debbie

It was 8:00 on a Friday night and Paula was shuffling through files and paperwork on her desk. Everybody in her office had pretty much left for the weekend, but she was still there working, trying to get ahead. She was a lawyer and was no stranger to working late on a Friday night especially when trying to become the youngest female partner in her firm. It was a noble and worthwhile goal, at least that's what she told herself everyday that she worked late.

She would work an extra two hours every day, but as hard as she worked, it was really the only thing she had in her life, except for a best friend and a few family members in Indiana. She wasn't married, she didn't have that great house with 2.5 kids and a dog and a cat like you were supposed to have by the time you reach 30 years of age. She had her career and it suited her well.

Janet, one of the other female lawyers in the Chicago law firm that Paula worked at was still at the office and as she was about to leave she came by Paula's office to say goodnight.

"Hey Paula," Janet said while standing in the doorway. "You still here working on Friday night; you should be out on a date or getting hammered tonight."

Paula laughed and replied. "I wish, but I have too much work to get done so my Friday is pretty much spent here with take out for dinner. Where you off to looking all spruced up?"

"I've got a date tonight with this really hot doctor. He's in private practice now so he can go out on Friday Nights."

"How cute is he?"

"I'll put it this way; he's got the body and the package of a Chip and Dale's dancer, the smoothness of James Bond, and the intellect of Noble Laureate."

"So basically you're waiting a few dates to jump his bones?"

"Hell after the first date, we talked for an hour, he poured on the charm, and then I couldn't take it anymore. I jumped his bones right then and there in the parking lot of the restaurant we were at. He ravished me in his car. Tonight we might actually make it to my place before the first hour is over."

"So I guess desert will be at your place tonight."

"And breakfast if I'm lucky! Anyway have a good weekend. I'll see you on Monday."

Paula couldn't help but laugh at her coworker then she felt sad for her because she didn't have the heart to tell her that this wonderful man wouldn't stick around much longer since they had already had sex a few times. After all he got what he wanted and maybe the fun would last for a little while, but it wouldn't be anything true. Then Paula felt sad not for her coworker anymore, but for her own circumstances because she didn't even have a man in her life that would ravish her in his car even if it was just for the night. Men need it pretty much every second of the day, but a woman needs it too even if for just a night so she can know what it means to have a little passion in her life. Paula sat back in her chair taking a sip of her diet coke with her solemn thoughts.

She missed having a man around even if it was a good friend that she couldn't stand to talk to, but just screw when she really needed it. It seemed like everybody around her could find someone. All of her friends were married and everybody she knew was dating on the weekends trying to find that perfect somebody. Seeing her coworker Janet all dolled up about to go out on a date with a really hot guy when she didn't deserve it. Janet had cheated on her first husband and every other man she had ever been with. It made Paula feel sad that she didn't have someone to go home to or go out with. She put down her pen and her diet coke and thought to herself, "fuck it."

It was a Friday night and she need to be out, not stuck in an office working, and the best person to be with was her best friend Debbie. He friend Debbie always understood her sadness and somehow her friend could always make her feel better. She called Debbie's Cell Phone.

Debbie saw who it was calling and answered. "Hey, sweet thing, what are you up to this Friday night?"

"Still at the office working... as usually."

"Honey, you work too damn hard, you should be out with me tonight. The action is great tonight!

"Really, where are you?"

"I'm actually at that old college joint of ours, The Matador."

"Wow, I haven't been there in a while. Is it still filled with young good looking college men."

"Honey, that's why I'm here. It's not for the beer, I'll tell you that."

"Well, I'm leaving here now and I need a drink, really I need to get over my melancholy blues tonight."

"Oh, its one of those Friday nights. The only way to get over that besides cookies and ice cream is whisky and younger men."

"You're on, I'll see in you in thirty minutes"

Paula packed up her things and said goodbye to the cleaning crew as she walked out the door. She knew The Matador well and it was one of those places that always got her through the rough times. It got her through law school and the owners were always nice if I do say so myself. I'm never short of philosophical advice for life, which was something every law student needs and it's one thing that makes me great to be around, at least that's what I think. It's also part of The Matador's charm. It was also something Paula looked forward to every time she was in here and it might just be something that she needed tonight.

Paula arrived about thirty minutes later just like she said she would and Debbie was there to greet her with a drink, something with whisky in it knowing that her friend was in desperate need of it. The place was jumping as usual for a Friday night. So as Paula walked through the door she was met by her friend who was flirting with both young men and women. Debbie led Paula to the back of the bar to the booth not too far from the jukebox that was playing *Shook Me all Night Long* by ACDC.

Debbie looked at Paula with a half smile and asked her. "So what's up girlfriend, why the sudden urge to blow off work and come party with me on a Friday Night?"

"Do you ever wonder how we got here," Paula asked.

"How we got to The Matador tonight or how we got to this point in our life because I'm a little drunk and confused by what you're asking."

"I took a cab to get here, but I meant how we got here in our lives."

"Is this because you just turned thirty this year and you're not married with those 2.5 kids, a dog, a cat, and a house with a yard?"

"It's a little bit about that, but I'm really wondering how I got this point in my life and if there is something wrong with me."

"Okay, what really happened tonight?"

"It's not just one thing, I work all the time, I'm hardly ever home, I can't remember the last time I took a vacation, I can't remember the last time I had sex that wasn't with myself. But the one thing that really started this was the office slut who keeps finding men to go out with her. I can't even get one to look at me."

"Paula she's a whore so of course she demeans herself and throws away all accountability just to get a man to look at her. It's the next step up from just showing your tits to every innocent bystander on the street."

Paula laughed and said. "I know, but more than ever I feel like I'm truly failing at something and maybe it's just because I'm officially thirty instead of approaching thirty with a slight chance of a reprieve."

"Honey all women feel that way when they hit thirty and that's why we flirt with younger men. We have officially become the older woman fantasy and women like us deserve someone with lots of energy. Also look at the bright side; you'll be hitting your sexual peak soon."

Paula gave Debbie a dirty look and replied in a sarcastic tone. "Oh good so it will be even better as I have battery-operated sex with myself."

"Debbie laughed and said. "That's why you need a younger man for a night and this place is filled with them."

As soon as she said that Debbie saw a friend walk through the door and got up to go say hi. Paula sipped her drink and thought to herself maybe Debbie was right. Maybe happiness could come from a detachment of serious emotion and with the kind of fun that happens only for a night without the getting to know someone in order to have intimacy. Paula started to think about her life from her child to the last twelve years that she had been in Chicago for school and a career.

Paula was from Kokomo Indiana, not a small town, but not a big city either. Her mother had her when she was only 19 years old. Her mother got pregnant from the first guy that had ever told her that he loved her. A few years later her mother met a man at the local factory that she worked at and after a month dating she married him deciding that her own happiness was not as important as finding a father for her little girl. The real father was not in the picture and he would have been too stoned anyway to make a good father.

In all honesty, according to Paula, her stepfather never really liked her and she never liked him. From the first day they all lived together as some misguided nuclear family Paula never got along with her stepfather; there were a few happy moments she had with him, but all in all their relationship was never good. However Paula did have a little brother, which she absolutely adored. When she was eighteen and had graduated high school she got a scholarship to the University of Chicago and took it moving away as soon as she was graduated so her stepfather couldn't have a say in where she went to college. Over the course of four years in college she very rarely went home even though it was only a few hours away. She chose to stay in Chicago for summers talking extra classes and working her way through the big city so she wouldn't have to return home as somebody who could not hack it in the big city. Paula studied political science and philosophy, it was in those classes that she met her best friend Debbie, she was masquerading as a philosopher and activist, but really Debbie was just there for the excitement and to be the life of the party. Eventually Paula went to law school at the University of Chicago and started practicing at a small law firm working harder every year to make partner by the time she was 30 years old. She was still working for it.

     Paula had never really known a normal relationship before, The two times she had been in love with someone turned out to be a disaster and one of those people was still around to a degree even if he didn't know it. She always seemed to fall for a guy that would screw her over in some way or didn't really love her even though he might have said he did. Somehow she would always be attracted to a guy that was bad for her and that she could never have a good relationship with. Truth be told, Paula had never had a good relationship with a man, from her real father walking away when she was born, to her stepfather who never really loved her, and to the man she was currently in love with but could never have because he was married.

Even in college her so-called college sweetheart turned out to be engaged to another woman while having his flings with Paula. Her entire history of a man's love for her was tragedy in the purest sense. Paula could never find something normal because she never knew what it really was. When it would come into her life she would run away from it never looking back. All of these thoughts ran through her mind as she sipped her drink and even though unlike most people she knew what her problem was but didn't know how to fix it.

Debbie was different though for she was almost the complete opposite. She was feisty, and full of life and completely under the misconception that she had any kind of problems with intimacy and relationships. Paula was always envious of that because it took a special kind of ego and stubbornness to live under that cloud of misguided notions. Maybe that's one of the reason she loved Paula so much even though Debbie was in love with her and not in a plutonic way. Hey what is one to do, friends aren't supposed to be perfect, they're just supposed to be there for you when you need them the most.

Debbie came back over to the booth and said to Paula "This Place has a lot of action here tonight, just not my kind of action. I keep striking out tonight."

"At least you get some kind of action on a weekly basis."

"If you had decided to be a lesbian with me then we wouldn't be having this problem."

"I still love you though."

"Prove it, buy me a drink."

Both women laughed over the sarcastic nature of their relationship. Some time in college Debbie had finally figured out that she was gay and loved women more. Paula had gone through an experimental phase back then as she was going back and forth with her two-timing college sweetheart. She didn't know if she could like women more and at one point when she was really, really hating men she decided to find out. She and Debbie would sleep together for a two weeks and then Paula's experiment was over. She figured out that she loved men more even though they were bastards. Debbie was mad for a while, but they realized that their friendship was too important to let the difference in sexuality get between them. Although Debbie was still a little bit in love with Paula and in joking manner let her know that if she decided to be a lesbian she would always be there waiting for her.

"So what's going on with the married guy," asked Paula.

"Still love him and still can't have him, at least not in the way I want," Paula replied.

"At least you've decided not to have an affair with him anymore. Its one ten commandment you're not breaking so it's a step in the right direction."

"I guess, but it doesn't make it any less awkward at the firm when I see him and he knows I'm still in love with him."

About two years ago Paula had started something that she thought she never would do. She fell in love with a married man and had an affair. He was a one of the partners at the firm and he was also of the lawyers who had mentored her when she was first hired 5 years before. His name was Lance and he was ten years older than she was, but he was funny, smart, and somehow made her feel better about who she was as a person and a lawyer. Perhaps it was because he paid attention to her when nobody else would and he was nice to her when most men were not.

    At first it all started innocently like most affairs when he was having trouble in his marriage. Lance and his wife were trying to work things out, but he still found comfort in the arms of someone who adored him and welcomed him with open arms. Both of them didn't care about morality. She was lonely while needing a man to make her feel good and he needed some confused notion of comfort to make him feel better about the choices he made that had made him miserable. The affair lasted for over a year, it lasted through late nights working together that ended at her place and weekends together that he told his wife were work related.

    All through the affair she would cling to the hope that he would leave his wife for her and even though he made promises they would only be lies. One day Paula received the honest to God truth of who he really was. He never planned on leaving his wife and she wasn't the first woman that had worked at the firm he had an affair with. Through all the nice qualities that were seen on the surface he really wasn't a good person. Paula would end the affair, but she still loved him even today and the small hope was still there that he would leave his wife for her. She didn't say much to him anymore, but was still nice to him and she would even help him out at work. Really it wasn't much different than before the affair except he didn't sleep in her bed together.

Because Paula was still in love with Lance she never dated anymore and let work be her life even though Debbie always tried to get her to go out with somebody that she knew. Sometimes Debbie would suggest a man who was recently divorced. Sometimes it was somebody who needed a brief fling because she didn't want Paula to be sex deprived. Sometimes it was a great guy she knew who was thinking about leaving his wife that needed somebody to help him along so of course she thought of Paula. That last category was bad, but at least Paula would be used to the scenario. All of them turned out to be disasters.

As Debbie and Paula were talking more about her little problem with married men and Paula was bringing her up to date on that little saga a couple of gentlemen walked in the bar. One of them took notice of Paula while smiling at her.

She smiled back thinking about how she knew them because they looked familiar. The two men took a seat at the bar and started conversing with the regulars; they apparently knew everybody and came in the bar on a regular basis.

Debbie looked at Paula who was not paying attention and said. "I think its time for you to try the online dating thing again."

Paula gave her a dirty look and replied. "Oh know, I'm not going through that again!"

"Why not, you can meet men that way, not all of them are good, but there's got to be a few that would work out."

"At this point I'm totally convinced that every man who puts a profile on a personal site is lying."

"What about that Net Harmony, you know it was invented by that doctor guy who forces the people to be honest through the questions that are asked and then they match you with someone based on your answers."

"It's still on the internet, right?"

"Yeah, but you have to be honest in the questions they ask you on this website for it to work."

"Oh, okay because people never lie when asked questions about themselves on the internet especially at a place that has harmony in the title."

"You're just going to be negative aren't you? I know all the other personal sites you tried didn't work for you, but this Net Harmony might just be the one."

"How do you know that this doctor guy who invented is even a real doctor, he could be a real doctor like Dr. Phillip who just sounds intelligent with his clever southern euphemisms like 'you're like a string without a shoe.' It sound like a scam to me just like those other sites who try to make you feel better by telling you that there is somebody out there for you and we can help you can find them for $30 a month. Besides I don't think real love exists for $30 a month."

Debbie started laughing knowing that Paula was right in her observations about online dating and she knew that out of all the people who had tried it Paula deserved to be disgruntled about the process. Over the last few years knowing that they were both slowly approaching thirty Paula and Debbie set out to find their better halves anyway they could and the new way to do it was online dating. If you were willing to really find love then all you had to do was put yourself out there for everybody to get you know you in the exciting world of cyberspace. You put a profile of yourself, with a few pictures, a charismatic tag line, and you have that certain one find you, at least that's what the brochures say. Paula and Debbie were always amused by them.

    The truth was Paula had tried it, not necessarily wholeheartedly, but she had tried it. With Debbie's help Paula put herself out there on the dating market. Debbie made her sound interesting in her profile, someone that craved adventure instead of somebody that was more devoted to work than having a social life and enjoyed a bottle of wine more at home than being out of public. It worked to a point, but her experiences were nothing less than comical and sometimes just disturbing. Paula had told herself that she would try it and just see if it could work. She got more than she bargained for.

    Everyone she met through the site turned to out to be more than just a little crazy or sad and pathetic; they turned out to be tragic cases of humanity clinging to some last desperate attempt of finding that so called true love. Truth be told, the people that Paula met were only acting the part of people who wanted to find true love, but really they wanted the appearance of someone who hadn't completely given up yet, not that Paula was much different. Sometimes the mere appearance of something can seem like the truth. She found men who still had mother issues, me who were trying out religion to convince themselves that they weren't horrible human beings, and men that still had a few mother issues to work out, not too far off from the Norman Bates type, at least that's what it felt like on a date with these men. The mother issues have to be mentioned twice because that's what Paula mostly got with the men she found on those personal sites. Debbie looked at Paula with her sarcastic smile and replied. "Some of the men you've went out with through an online service were not that bad. And how 'bout the guy who was close to his mother, at least he was family oriented."

"You mean the guy who brought his mother along on our first few date. I'm sorry, but I think it's a bit creepy especially when she made him put his napkin like a bib so he could eat ice cream."

"All right then, how about the guy who was really outgoing and like to role play. That's a good thing and wasn't he a TV actor."

"He was a schizophrenic with multiple personalities. One of them just happened to be an actor. It also turns out he was married with two kids at home and just for fun he wouldn't take his medication then he would go out for the weekend to live a psychotic double life."

"Okay so few guys turned out to be crazy, that doesn't mean if you keep trying you won't find a good man."

"Let's face it, it's a lost cause and the only good man I've ever found was someone that I can't have. Despite everything he is still a good person, he just makes a few mistakes from time to time."

Debbie shook her head and laughed then she said to Paula. "Then you my friend are completely lost and a night with a younger man could be the cure." Paula laughed at her friend because she knew that Debbie was just trying to help. Debbie said. "Paula, I'll say this, it could always be worse. The other day I ran into Jen Anderson and she was still with that redneck boyfriend she's been dating for years. You know the wife beater that always has the Coors Lt. in one hand."

"No, Way I haven't seen her in years and I can't believe she would still be with that guy. How did he not ever end up in jail for assault they way he was always carrying on about how he was going to kick someone's ass?"

"We all go through our stupid times, everyone of us, even the smart ones like Jen. I'll never forget the time he said that women were only good for one thing, being in the kitchen birthing babies."

"He just proves that women are smarter than men, but then again monkeys are smarter than he is."

They both laughed and after ordering some more drinks Paula turned the subject of the conversation onto Debbie. She knew how her friend really was. Paula would wear her misery as a badge of honor, Debbie would become more flamboyant in her actions just to hide the fact that she was hurting inside. Debbie wanted to find that special someone just like anybody else, but even she had problems with that so she flirted and toyed with other's emotions just to amuse herself. Paula asked her friend. "Are you ever going to find someone to settle down with?"

"Are you kidding, I'm in the same boat as you when it comes to finding someone to truly commit. The only difference is the women I seem to find are still confused on whether they're gay or not. I'm just their little experiment. I'm not lucky enough to find someone who still married. I find the women that are like you."

"At least I can finally admit that I like men and I'm not stringing you along with my sexual confusion."

"That's true, but I still think if you were a lesbian things would be a whole lot easier between us."

"Another few years of not being able to find someone I might have to reconsider my sexuality, but in the mean time I still like men. No matter how bad I get treated I still like them."

"Online dating can help you shift through the bad men easier."

"What is you obsession with online dating. What makes it any easier than meeting people by accident? Meeting people by accident happens all the time; the guys I've been in love I've met by accident. Our parents, our grandparents they met each by accident even if it was through a mutual friend and if it worked for them then I think it can work for me."

"Bravo for you, but if you really think that," Debbie replied in a serious tone. "Then you can't let the misery of not finding someone be an excuse especially when you've never gone after it before."

"Counselor, I will concede my point and agree with you. However, I can't promise that I won't be miserable, but it's my misery and I don't have to show it to anyone. I don't know what accidents wait for me around the corner, but the only hope I have is that it will be good. With that said I'm going to the bathroom."

"Then I'll go flirt with some more guys just to make their night miserable because they can't have me or watch me with another woman."

Paula got up and went to the bathroom. The restrooms were around a corner from where her booth was and as she was leaving the bathroom she came around the corner and bumped into a guy who was still holding his drink. The drink landed on her as they bumped into each. The man immediately apologized for to her as she was dripping a whisky sour down her white blouse, which made it look like she was going to start a wet t-shirt contest in The Matador. As she looked up to scream an obscenity to him she recognized him. It was the man at the bar that was looking at her as if he knew her; it was Richard, Jack and Jen's brother that she had gone to college with. She looked at him and said in an angry tone "Richard Anderson, after all these years are you still making it a habit to piss me off. Honestly can't you watch where you're going and who brings a drink with them to the bathroom anyway?"

"Paula Simpson," He replied. "Getting you mad is not really that exciting to me anymore. Just the thought of it is a waste of time and as for my drink I don't have to explain to you what my drinking habits are, I'm not under oath so it's not any of your business."

"Still a smart ass I see," she replied as she tried to dry off.

"You're still a tough as nails bitch that's always spoiling for a fight."

"I deal with jerks like you all day, I have to be just to get ahead. Richard was about to say something. Paula replied. "Don't say it. You're already on my shit list."

"I wasn't even thinking it, just shows how much you know about me."

"I know you're still a jerk."

"Maybe, but I pull it off in a loveable charming way, that's why I still have friends."

"Yeah, sounds like you're already drunk tonight. You've got your delusions of grandeur."

"I'd watch what you say, I know you're a lawyer and you never know when your mistakes might be blasted all over the front page of the newspaper after talking with me."

"You mean the front page of the sports section... I know you're a sports writer and you would never cover anything I do."

"I know you know that; I just wanted to prove that you'd been keeping up with me all these years."

"Don't flatter yourself with trying to be smart, you don't have that kind of talent."

Richard started laughing because he knew how Paula was; you see they had a history together and even though they wouldn't admit it they knew each other better than most people. Ever since college they had to challenge each other and they knew had to infuriate each other well. It was something a loving couple only knows. However, their story is for another time.

Richard smiled at Paula and said. "Well since we're both here in our old college hangout let me buy you a drink that you don't have to wear. Besides I need another one anyway."

"It's the least you can do; I should get a fancy dinner at Bergoffs from you.

How come you still hang out here, still trying to hit on 21 year olds?"

"The Matador is a special place and the best place to be on the weekend besides Wrigley Field. Anyway I couldn't get away from Trinidad, I need a bartender that knows what I like to drink and has great advice. Lord knows I can't afford a shrink."

"Well admitting you need one is the first step to recovery."

They both laughed and went back to her booth. I made Debbie a drink while she was standing at the bar and then looked over at Paula and Richard while smiling. Debbie just gave Mike a dirty look because she never really liked him and he returned one to her as well. Both of them noticed what I was looking at and had the same dumbfounded look I did while staring at Richard and Paula.

I have always been amused at the accidental happenings that occur in my bar. I said to Debbie, another person I have known for over ten years since she was in college hanging out at his place almost every night."I see Richard and Paula bumped into each other again after all these years."

Debbie said to him. "Yes and it looks like another round with those two.

Oh and look they're insulting each other as usual."

Mike replied to her statement. "You would think those two would have had enough of each other even after all these years."

"You know what that means when all you can do is insult each other, you're falling in love," I said with a sarcastic smile. So in the end that's how it started again for Richard and Paula.

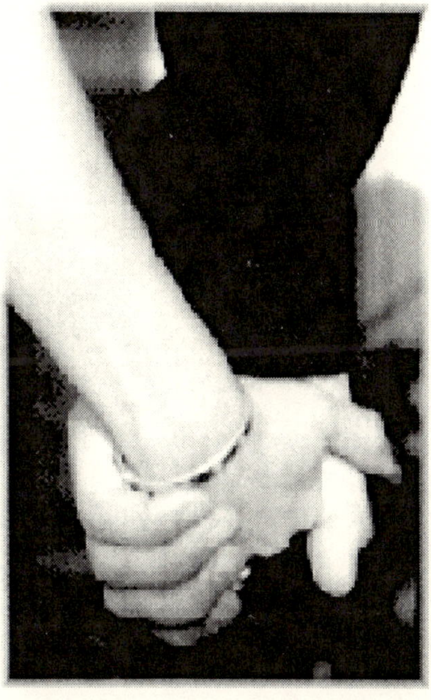

4

Jen, Jarrod, and Sam

Jen continued to stare in the mirror at the black eye that had been there since yesterday. She had never had one before; her boyfriend had never hit her before. Jen wasn't unaware of abusive relationships, her parents had one and her father was the physical type when it came to discipline, but the harsh world seems to be clearer when it happens to you. Her boyfriend Sam had shoved her in anger before when they got into a fight, but no matter how much he lost his temper he never got this bad. Jen never thought he was capable.

She had been dating Sam for six years, they came from different worlds, and what seemed like different times because his views could be a little old fashioned. Old fashioned might be putting it lightly she thought to herself especially after what happen in their last fight. She was from Chicago with two older brothers and mixture of faith and liberalism. Sam on the other hand was from Texas where all he had were two sisters, a very conservative mother and father, and a narrow-minded view of how the world should be. However, he had values and was a gentleman most of the time with faith being a central part of his life. It was this quality that first attracted Jen to Sam and the fact that when they first met he was her knight in shining armor when she needed one.

As Jen got ready for her work day she tried her best to cover up the love that Sam had written all over her face. She loved him, but after six years of being together, she didn't know the reasons why anymore. They had been living together for 4 years now and the last year or so had been the most turbulent. They had planned on getting married and convinced themselves that someday they would, perhaps that's why they stayed together even when things were really bad. Jen wasn't ready to give up on somebody that she would spend the rest of her life with or so she told herself, but the thought had occurred more and more in the last year.

As she got ready she started to think back to how she ended up here, ended up with a boyfriend who was more temper than love and living in a place with broken lamps and dishes. It wasn't the type of place she expected to be, but she also knew that with any relationship you had to work at it. Although she always wondered when was the right time to finally leave? Unfortunately, it wasn't a clear-cut answer, not even for the smartest person in the world.

On her way to work she thought back to when she first met Sam and what made her fall for him. She met him in college one night when she was out with her friends at a club. Her boyfriend at the time wasn't a good guy and tended to be very selfish, never caring much for what she wanted to do. So it happened that she was out for the evening with her friends, a girls night out, and after telling him that she was going to be out alone with her friends he showed up to the club that she was at looking for her because he wanted her to be with that night.

They argued in front of everybody and when he shoved her a guy from across the room saw what happened and came over to intervene. The guy turned out to be Sam and he stopped her boyfriend from doing anything else even going as far as to punch him a few times until all her boyfriend could do was bleed and run out the door. Sam was her hero that night and after she bought him a drink as a sign of thanks. That's when it started between them. At first, Sam was great; he was respectful doing things like holding the door open in a public place. He listened to her and did things with her even though he didn't like to do them. He was a family man and as they started dating one of the first things he wanted to do was meet her family.

Sam was a Texas boy, misplaced in Chicago, going to school and studying to be an engineer. He was out of place in the big city world that Jen had grown up in. All he knew was the country, oil fields, and ranching, but somehow through academics he ended up in a place like Chicago getting his education at one of the world's most prestigious engineering schools. None of that mattered to Jen,

Sam was nice and he treated her well, and that was all she needed to know. They started dating and getting serious, they made it all the way through college and his post-graduate education. However, about year into their relationship when all the new dust of romance had settled she discovered his temper and male chauvinist attitudes toward women.

    At first Jen thought it was just the good ol' boy in him and part of his upbringing; something she could overlook because people could change over time and she was used to men with tempers. She had a father with a temper. It was more than that, after six years she finally realized that he saw women as second-class citizens, and that their place was at a man's side.. The most disturbing thought, however, was his belief that in certain instances a man had the right to hit a woman to keep her in line if needed. Sam rarely ever hit her, sometimes he would shove her into a wall, but every time he was physical a mark was left on her. It was more than physical; it was emotional because it felt like that he was trying to destroy the woman she really was so he could remake her into what he wanted her to be.

In the beginning she was idealistic, she believed that as they got older he would change and the young man's attitude in him would go away with the coming of wisdom, age, and experience. They had their good moments even past the moments of anger when all he could do was be angry at her because she wouldn't marry him and settle down in Texas. She loved him though because he stayed in Chicago for her and when they moved in together, she actually thought that he would finally change. But no matter how idealistic and foolish she was in the six years they has been together he wouldn't change.

Jen got through the workday without anyone noticing her marks except by her best friend at work, Julie. The bruise that Sam had left was around her jaw and with enough make up and turning to the opposite direction of the mark when she talked to people did enough to keep people from noticing. She had made it through the day until about noon when Julie noticed the mark and asked her about it. Jen told her about the argument, about how Sam didn't want her hanging out with her girlfriends at The Matador anymore because he felt uncomfortable around her friends. When she said that she wasn't going to do that they argued. He got mad at her. forbidding her to be out alone with her friends, then he hit her.

During lunch, Julie got very serious with Jen. She wanted her to be completely honest and answer her question of why she loved Sam, of why she stayed with him, and if it they were the same reasons she had six years before. Jen couldn't answer the question, all she could do was think about it. That's when Julie looked at her with serious look on her face and scolding tone in her voice. "If you have to think about the answer then you don't love him. If the answer isn't on the tip of your tongue, waiting to be said aloud like its instinct then you don't love him."

It was that statement that stuck with Jen and she couldn't get her mind off of it; it would stay with her for days like a splinter buried deep on the tip of her finger. A few days later Jen went over to her parent's house to have Sunday lunch with her family. She hadn't seen Sam in a few days -he was still cooling off, and probably drunk somewhere with what few friends he actually had. She was the last one to arrive and although most of her family's attention was on her brother Jack, trying to console him over his divorce being finalized her mother immediately took notice of the bruise on her face. Her mother made a loud comment about directing everybody's attention to it.

Although Jen would try to tell everybody that it wasn't what it looked like, it was just an accident that happened at work, her mother knew better. She was a victim too, a victim of a stubborn and cruel man's anger. After her brothers and father went into the living room to drink and watch football Jen's mother kept her in the kitchen so they could have one of those mother and daughter talks. Jen tried to get out of it, but her mother was a very stubborn Danish woman so there was no getting out of it. Her mother sat her down at the kitchen table and asked her directly.

"So how are you and Sam doing?"

"We're doing fine mother, same as always."

"Uh, huh-I can see that, it's written all of your face."

"What are you talking about, there's nothing wrong with my face."

"Oh there was another reason why you're wearing so much makeup. Honestly, what was it this time that set

Sam off, you having a life of your own outside of him?"

"Fine, if you want to know the truth, he hit me. We had an argument and he hit me."

"What was the argument about?"

Jen started to cry a little bit, she turned her head away from her mother trying to hide what her mother already knew. Mothers always know the truth; whether we want to admit it somehow they always seem to know the things we never want them to know. Finally, Jen collected her words and replied to her mother "You were right about everything."

He mother reached across the table and hugged her and then told her."

"I'm not trying to be right about everything and I'm certainly not trying to be the one that told you so like your father. All I want is my daughter to be happy and to have a loving relationship like she deserves."

"I know. The truth is Sam is not the person he used to be and no, he doesn't want me to have a life outside of him. I went out with my friends and he threw a fit because I wasn't with him for some business function that night. His function was more of a guy's night out anyway."

"I take it he yelled at you and when you trying to speak in some adult like manner that's when he lost it and hit you."

"That's exactly what happened, how did you know?"

"Because it always happens that way with a man that just wants to control you and can't stand the fact that you have a mind of your own. I should know it took quite a few years for your father and me to come to an understanding; you know how controlling he can be."

"Yeah, but how did you straighten him out."

"Well it wasn't easy and there were a few times in some heated arguments that he lost control and slapped me. You may not remember because you were pretty young."

"I don't remember that, but I remember him being quite the disciplinarian. He never spared us from spankings when we were really in trouble."

Her mom smiled and said."You're father had a pretty bad temper when we first got married and he had some pretty wacky ideas when it came to a woman's role in life. One night when I was cooking dinner and we got into an argument over something I can't even remember, but he threw something at me and I dumped dinner out of the frying pan threatening to beat him with it. He came toward me, testing me and I broke a few fingers on his hand with the pan as he tried to get a hold of me. After that we had an understanding, if we ever get into a serious argument where we felt like hitting one another we just walk away because if we didn't somebody was going to get hurt."

Jen started laughing at her mother and was a little surprised because she had never heard that story before. She could remember her parents having some really serious arguments where they would get into each other's face while cursing one another, but then they would walk away and not speak to each other for the rest of the day. Jen just thought it was normal with two stubborn people; you had to get away before the fire and anger would completely erupt. Arguing was fine because it was a warning that something serious was about to happen. Jen asked her mother. "Is that what you have to do in order to make a man the man you want them to be?"

"I'm not saying that you have to do it exactly that way, but men have to be straightened out if you're going to make a relationship work."

"What do you think I should do about Sam?"

"Honey I can't tell you what to do when it comes Sam. You have to figure that out on your own, but you should already know what to do."

"Do you think Sam can change?"

"I believe in all possibilities, but has he tried to change in any way over the last six years?

"Not really, it seems like he got worse."

"As we get older we are supposed to be getting better as a person, not taking two steps back for every one step we take."

"I've thought about it several times... you know about breaking up and moving on with the rest of my life, but after six years it just seems that..."

Her mother cut her off and replied. "That you've made too much of a commitment and should just stick it out."

"Yeah, I feel like the best part of my life has been with him and why should I stop. Maybe we have more together."

"Honey, you've had one part of your life together, but you still have a lot of years. Some relationships are never meant to last even if they've been going on for a long time. Can you honestly say that this one was meant to be for the rest of your life?"

Jen sighed for a moment and then she replied. "I don't know anymore and it used to be something I knew without any doubt. I have to say, I never thought that this relationship could come to an end....that I would have any doubts about my future with this man."

"I know how you feel; there were quite a few years with your father when I didn't know if we were going to make it. Somehow we did though and here we are today. If not, you and your brothers would be children of divorced parents"

Jen smiled which she had not done in a while since this whole thing with Sam had begun. She asked her mother with a curiosity that had not been there in a long time and this time she was really searching for answers instead of just accepting things as they are because people had always said that it's just the way it is.

"How did you guys make it work?"

"We fought for it and we fought hard for it. Your father and me both realized that despite all of our disagreements and lack of common interests at the end of the day we were better with each other. Part of that came from the fact that we challenged each other and in every relationship you have to challenge each other in different ways just to keep things interesting and exciting."

"You know mom, I can't remember a time that I had that with Sam."

"Then you have your answer of whether or not you should stick it out with him. You can't have a relationship with someone who can't keep you on your toes or keep you humble in some way. Of course any man that continually hits you when he's angry is not worth it."

"Why didn't you tell me that before?"

"It's not my place to tell you that, you should be able to figure that on your own. I can have my opinion, but you're an adult now and you should make these decisions on your own."

Jen smiled as her mother gave her a smile that said everything was going to be okay and then she reached across the table to hug her mother. Sometimes in order to make a decision we just need to hear it from someone that we trust, someone that we can rely on because they're always there for us.

It had been a week since Sam had left and all that time she hadn't spoken to him once. She spent the week thinking about the past and the future, and she weighed her options by creating a list of pro and cons on a legal pad just like her father had taught her. As it turned the cons were more and she still didn't want to believe. She thought to herself that it was cold and heartless to make those decisions regarding relationships, but it was the only logical way she could make the decision. However, it didn't stop her from feeling a touch of the blues for the decision she about to make because a part of her life was ending in sadness.

At the end of the week Sam finally returned so they could sort things out. He was calm and he was nice, something he hadn't been in while. Sam and Jen sat at their kitchen table like rational adults starting to talk and so they talked about the future and where they saw themselves in the years to come. Even though they didn't want to admit it what they saw was different and to their surprise there was no anger, just the sadness of the end to come.

Jen asked him Sam "Did you ever see us making it and growing old together?"

"At one time I did, but the way you've been acting the last year or so I don't know anymore," he replied.

"Say what you want," Jen replied in an angry tone. "I've only changed because the things I want are different now and being treated like shit by you isn't one of them."

"What happened to you, we used to want the same things."

"Maybe we never did and you only thought we did because you never saw my life outside of yours."

"I don't think that's true."

"Then you believe what you want, but you are not as gallant as you once were, you're not the good man you used to be and I can't live with that anymore just because I'm afraid to be alone."

Sam finally got angry. His tact and polite demeanor ceased to be because now he was hurt. Sam replied to her in an angry tone "well then fuck you, you've become the cold heartless bitch you never wanted to be."

"Only because you've made me that way!"

Sam got up from the table and pushed his chair out of the way in anger. He didn't want to hear it, he didn't want to hear the truth that somebody he loved thought he was a horrible guy and not worth being with. He replied to her. "I don't know why we can't just go back to the way things used to be when we first met."

Jen while shedding a few tears said. "Because we're different people and you're not the same person you used to be. You're worse."

"I think you've gone crazy as you got older, just like you're crazy family."

"You know I thought this was going to be hard because I kept telling myself that it was worth fighting for, but the insults and the way you're acting has made this a lot easier. I done with you and I don't want to ever see you again."

"You'll regret it and you know that you will never find someone like me."

"I hope I never do. You may think that I'll regret it, trust me I won't... for the first time in six years I won't'"

With that said she walked away despite his angry pleadings . She told him that she would be gone for a few days and he could move his stuff out. As soon as Jen said that she gave him one last look and found to courage to walk out the door and leave forever.

Sam moved his stuff out and left for good; he didn't necessarily leave her alone, but he was moved out. Sometimes he would call her and ask her to come back to him, sometimes he would run into her at her favorite coffee place trying nonchalantly to get her to see that he was the best thing for her. For a while it was hard for her because it was the first time in six years that she was alone. The hardest part was sleeping in a bed alone and for the first few nights that Sam was gone she didn't get much sleep. But she would find an answer to her problem, as people tend to do even when they're not looking.

 One day when Jen got back to her apartment from a long day at work she was checking her mail and there he was, standing there alone. He was the mysterious good-looking neighbor that she had only spoken a few words to in passing. He lived a few doors down from her and his name was Brian. Jen didn't know anything about him except that he was attractive and always had something funny to say. As they were checking their mail Jen decided to take a chance and start a conversation with Brian. That conversation turned into dinner that night inside his apartment.

 She found out all about him and realized they had more in common that she ever imagined in her brief fantasies of him while passing him at the mailboxes or on the elevator. The most important thing they had in common was being part of a bad breakup that left them devastated and broken hearted while not being able to trust the opposite sex. Something pretty common among people both of them realized.

Of course over dinner that night they told each other their sad sordid tales of love and loss as they each found comfort in the indiscriminant affections of a stranger. So it became no surprise that they would end up sleeping together that night and for the most part almost every night after that. They would trade their time between each other's residences so they didn't have to be alone, but not having to commit to something that they didn't have the strength for anymore.

Sam was out of Jen's life for good, but she found his replacement in the unsuspecting rebound of a neighbor that she could disclose her thoughts to, but never her heart. Giving her heart away to Brian would require taking a chance and finding something of hope, but there was none to be found. For Brian he never asked for love from her because he had none to give and their routine lasted for eleven months.

One night when Jen and Brian were staying up late watching TV there was something that had been bothering her for a while so she asked her question instead of keeping silent. Jen looked over at Brian and asked him. "Do you think you'll ever get a second chance?"

"What do you mean, a second chance at what," he asked her.

"Do you think you'll ever find love again?"

"Why are you asking, is there something you want to tell me?"

"I don't want to be that girl and I know that we always agreed that there would be no strings attached. That's the way we've always left it and I'm fine with that, but we've been doing this for almost a year now. Haven't you wondered about anything?"

Brian sighed and thought for a moment while trying to choose his words carefully then he replied. "Are you saying that you want more from this or did you meet somebody that you want a real relationship with?"

"I didn't meet anybody, but I am wondering about you and me because we sleep together almost every night trading out time between each other's places and acting like a typical couple. We do get along and we enjoy being with one another, doesn't that mean something?"

"Sure it does, it means we're likeminded people, but I don't think it means what you think it does."

"I'm not asking you to meet my family or for a ring, but I think we've become more than just casual acquaintances getting together for some bedroom fun and definitely more than an extended one night stand. Do you see us having more of a relationship than what we have now?"

Brian thought for a moment and said to her. "All things are possible, but what's wrong with what we have now. Do you want to be in a real relationship again? Do you really want to do it with me?"

Jen gave Brian a dirty look and replied. "I don't see why anybody wouldn't want to be in a relationship with your level of excitement. I think we are beyond just having someone nearby so we don't have to be alone and I think we need to talk about it."

Brian gave her a heartfelt look and replied. "Then let's talk about it, but I think we should do it when we've both have had a chance to really think about what we want."

What he said sounded fake to her, but she got Brian to talk about the issue at hand and for right now it was good enough. They both went to bed and didn't give what they had talked about another thought. Jen and Brian just went on with their routine for the next few weeks without talking about it. Jen waited for Brian to bring the subject up so they could talk about it, but her suspicion eventually came true - he ignored their conversation and went on with his life.

The next weekend Jen was out with her friend Julie at The Matador and so through the course of the evening the subject of her and Brian came up. Julie asked her what was going on and if Jen had finally had the talk with him. The Talk, which eventually happens in every relationship no matter what kind it is, can be the most devastating part because it's where the real truth comes out and we can't get by anymore with the silence that never speaks what we don't want to her.

Jen didn't know how to begin to answer that question, but the look on her face gave Julie her answer. So Julie asked Jen. "So how did the talk go?"

"Can't you tell by my lack of excitement," Jen answer her friend.

"I can't say that I'm surprised, Brian doesn't seem like the type of guy that would drop down to his knees and commit."

"What makes you even say that?"

"You had to bring the subject up and he still won't talk about it with you. It doesn't sound like a man that can ball up and be a man by being totally honest with you."

"I guess you have a point, but still..."

"But what, he's a nice guy that doesn't treat you bad so he must be worth it-is that what you were going to say."

"If you already know what I am going to say then why do I need to say it out loud!"

"That's what friends are for-we say the things that you don't want to say so you don't have to sound like a complete idiot."

"Is that so?"

"Yeah and friends also buy a friend a drink when they need one, isn't that right Trinidad?"

I was at the bar standing over by where they were sitting just listening to the conversations that were going on and offering my two cents where it was needed like a good bartender. Truth be told I always thought of himself as the workingman's psychologist-someone who gave great advice for the price of a drink. So I responded in kind to the question.

"Julie your absolutely right and what better place to buy a drink than at my bar."

The girls laughed as they gave me their drink order and as I made their drinks right in front of them. Julie replied to Jen. "Look I'm not trying to make you feel bad tonight and I know that the past year hasn't been easy for you after Sam, but ask yourself what are you really looking for?"

"At this point in my life all I really want is someone to come home to, someone to spend time with, someone to listen to me, someone to hold me when I need it, and for someone to not break my heart."

I gave Jen a smile and before Julie could respond I said. "If that's all you really want then I suggest you get a dog and never fall in love again."

"What are talking about," Jen asked.

"What I'm saying is if you want to be in love then you have to risk your heart being broken, if you don't want that to happen then don't fall in love because you can't have one without the other-it's a two sided coin, never a one sided coin."

Julie started laughing and replied to me. "That's a good philosophy where did you come up with it?"

"Being married for forty years, it's just something you learn along the away and besides I laugh every time I hear about someone thinking they can be happy with that 'friends with benefits' scenario. It's just a cheap excuse so you don't have to make a commitment and to avoid not being alone."

Jen gave me a dirty look while Julie started Laughing. I didn't even know what was going in Jen's life, but I always seemed to know the right thing to say at the right moment. At least that's what I get told.

Julie replied to Jen "Well, he seems to have your 'number' tonight, but you know he's right."

Jen looked at her friend and replied. "Like you have anything to talk about, remember that little fling you had with your coworker last year?"

"I remember my thing with Jim, but the difference between me and you is even though my thing with him was a one night stand that lasted for two weeks after that it was over and I never spoke to him again. Your thing with Brian has lasted eleven months and you still haven't even gone on date with him yet."

"I have to gone a date with him."

"Taking you to a rock concert out in the park just so you can fuck in a public place doesn't count – it's just a kinky 'sexcapade' in order to spice up your 'friends with benefits' relationship."

I asked Jen. "Is that the relationship you have with the current guy you're with?"

"Maybe," She replied. "But I am trying to make it more than just that, but let me ask you something Trinidad, what really wrong with it? It's a relationship that makes sense to a degree and you can't tell me that they don't have that kind a thing in Spain where you're from."

I gave her a serious look and replied. "We do have the kind of relationships in Spain where all you do is have sex, but never commit to a traditional relationship."

"See, I knew it and there shouldn't be any judgment towards me because of what I have with Brian."

"Let me finish," I said in a serious tone. "The relationship I'm talking is with a prostitute or a mistress. That's how you get to have the sex without the commitment."

Julie started laughing and Jen didn't know what to say because she knew I was right in a way. I smiled at her and said to her that she didn't need to say anything else. All the advice she really needed I gave and then walked off leaving her and Julie to discuss among things themselves.

Jen was at a loss for words, there was nothing she could say that would convince Julie or anybody else including herself that what she had with Brian was good thing. The truth is we all do stupid things so we don't have to be alone and as smart as Jen was she was no different.

Julie and Jen started to talk about other things, but before they got too far ahead Julie turned the conversation back onto Jen's love life. She replied to her friend. "By the way for I forget there is somebody I think you should meet."

"Not again with meeting someone," Jen replied back. "I think I should find a solution for the so called relationship I have now before meeting another guy."

"I actually wanted to introduce you two about a year ago, but you were still trying to figure out what to do with Sam and he was in a relationship as well, but he would be perfect for you."

"I'm not going on a blind date, that's even worse than online dating. At least with that I can somewhat figure out if the person is a serial killer by conversing with them online. With a blind date there is no way knowing until it's too late. "

"I wouldn't do a blind for you. Next week I am having a dinner party for my friend who's the author to celebrate the release of his new book. I was going to invite him and you can meet him there."

"What does this guy do? He's not some kind of former criminal is he?"

"Far from it, he's actually a police officer and he is a very nice guy with good values and he's very family oriented. He's also a huge Cub's fan that grew up on the Northside not too far from Wrigley Field so your brothers would like him."

Jen sighed and replied back. "If I'm there and he's there then I'll meet, but I'm not doing anything else beside that.

"Hey, it's your loss if it doesn't work out...I can honestly say he's a great guy and definitely the one for you."

"If he's such a great guy then why don't you go out with him?"

"You know me I have to go for the bad boy who will eventually screw me over. If I didn't have that in my life so I could complain then I wouldn't have anything to talk to you about and for you to tell me what not to do in a relationship. Let's face it you need me for that" Julie replied in with a laughter in her tone.

They both started laughing at the truth in Julie's comment and then finished their drinks before taking part in a game of darts with some of the younger men there who thought that there was no way a woman could beat them. It was a fun little game that Jen and Julie played because they were really good at darts and could easily take money from the young dumb guys that were over confident to play with clear heads. Besides Jen and Julie got to flirt and show their superiority by making men want what they couldn't have.

The next day Jen finally had her heart to heart talk with Brian about the type of relationship they had. She was finally honest about what she truly wanted. Jen liked Brian and could see a real relationship with him and for the most part he liked her, but not enough to really commit. As they were talking she asked him the question, the question of whether they could have a future together.

Brian thought about it for a moment, but in pure honesty he just told her that he couldn't do it. He couldn't go through that again and he wasn't ready to risk being hurt again. He explained that to her and no matter how much she wanted to hate him she couldn't, she understood. Jen didn't shed any tears nor did he. They smiled at one another and hugged then gave back each other's spare apartment keys. That was it, they promised to keep in touch but they both knew it was just something nice to say to one another and not make what happened between them any more awkward after they parted. They went back to their home and never saw each other again.

The next day Jen stopped at her usual place to pick up her morning coffee. It was a little coffee joint not too far from where she worked that had great artistic appeal with fresh brewed coffee and a simple layout for the busy commuter, but never had the commercial appeal as Starbucks. Jen stopped there every morning to get a cup and she knew everybody that worked there including some of the usual customers that were there every morning getting their coffee to go.

For about two weeks she had been seeing this guy there almost every morning getting a coffee to go. She never really noticed the customers except for the ones that she knew, but he was different; he had a genuine quality about him. He seemed nice and friendly with everybody, helpful to the older people that were there in the mornings and well liked by the employees.

Jen was not the type of person to just walk up to somebody and start talking to them, but she wanted to know what it was about him and her curiosity finally took over. She waited for the right moment to say something clever so she didn't seem like a complete idiot. When he was standing in line trying to figure out what to get after deciding to himself to try something new she leaned around the person in front of her to whisper an answer to him.

"You want just a basic cup of coffee with two sugars, cream, and a sprinkle of cinnamon-you can't go wrong with something basic added with a dash of Christmas."

"He looked at her with a curious look and replied. "Well my mother always told me to trust a kind and beautiful woman who knew had to make a great cup of coffee." Then that's what he ordered.

After Jen made her coffee order the gentleman walked over and asked her. "So how did you know what kind of coffee I liked? A basic cup of coffee with a dash of cinnamon just happens to be my favorite."

"I didn't," she replied. "You looked like you needed a little help and when it comes to getting a great cup of coffee always go with the basics but with a dash of holiday bliss. It's the kind of coffee my mother likes to make during Christmas."

"Then I would say you were taught well."

"My mother is one of those that truly knows best and I did learn well. So tell me something, I've seen you in here almost every day for the last two weeks and you seem to know everybody here like they're your best friend. Don't tell me you've been coming here for a while. I would've seen you here."

The gentleman laughed a little and said. "You're pretty perceptive, but the answer to your question is I'm one of those that really likes getting to know people so I'm friendly with everybody. It helps me in my job to know people."

"What do you do?"

"I'll tell you, but first I think we should introduce ourselves. I'm Jarrod."

"My name is Jen," she said as she gave him a smile.

"It's nice to meet you Jen. I'd ask you if you come here often, but you already answered what my line would be in trying to pick you up." He replied in a sarcastic tone.

"I don't think you're the type of guy that needs a line to pick up women, you seem friendly enough with people you meet, but not in a sleazy way."

"Good at least I have that going for me."

"I'm sure you have a lot more going for you." she said not trying to seem too flirtatious. "So what do you do?"

"I'm a police officer, detective actually. And you."

"I work in a bank and do a job that nobody understands; I work with statistics so it's a real numbers game in my job... so to speak."

"At least you don't get shot at."

"Have you been shot at?"

"Fortunately no, but I get to deal with interesting things on a daily basis. Also people act in two ways with me, very afraid to talk to me or extremely weird like with most women I have met. They get excited that I have a job that requires handcuffs. Once in a while I get a normal person to talk to-maybe that's why I am so friendly with people, I'm just trying to find more normal people.

"You're in Chicago, I don't really think that exists. The only people that are crazier than us are people from Wisconsin and Texas."

Jarrod started laughing and so they continued to talk with one another. They talked and got to know one another as strangers tend to do in the most peculiar of circumstances. They talked for so long that both them ended up being late to work, but not before the agreed to meet each other for coffee sometime.

Later that week Jen decided to go to her friend's party. She thought to her herself that it wouldn't be that bad and despite meeting a really nice guy during the week if she happened to meet another one that her friend was trying to set her up with what's the worst that could happen. The guy could turn out to be a creep, she would leave early, and just meet Jarrod for coffee sometime like they agreed. No harm, no foul she thought. The party was on a Saturday night and there were many people there just as Julie had said. Jen actually knew a lot of them.

About half hour into the party the person Julie had wanted Jen to meet arrived. Julie quickly got him a drink and went to find Jen who was sitting on the patio talking with some people she knew. Julie was trying to rush her matchmaking skills hoping that whatever magic she had would not fade away by the time she reached the back of the house.

She found Jen with and with Jarrod right behind her she called out to her friend to get her attention. Jen turned around and immediately saw Jarrod. She had a look of surprise and a feeling joy when looking at Jarrod.

Julie looked at Jen and replied. "Girl, this is the guy I wanted you to meet. His name is…"

"Jarrod," she said with a joyful tone. "His name is Jarrod."

Jarrod looked at her with the same look of surprise, he gave her a smile letting her know that he was glad to see her. Then he replied. "And your name is Jen, I think we've meet before."

Julie looked at the two of them who couldn't take their eyes off one another while smiling like giddy school children who were just let out for recess. Julie replied. "I guess you two already know each other?"

They both answered yes at the same time. Julie said. "Well I'll leave you two to talk, but just in case you both were wondering I have been trying to get you both to meet each other for the past year because as far as I am concerned you're perfect for one another."

Jen and Jarrod didn't even look at her as she finished her sentence. They just stared at one another smiling because for them the race was finally over. Julie walked off and left her friends alone to talk.

Jarrod asked her. "Did you know who I was when we met the other day?"

"No, Julie never described you; she just said I should meet you." Jen said.

"Well I guess we should just have our coffee date right here, no sense in waiting to find out if we're a perfect match."

"Why not. I think is going to get interesting especially if a mutual friend of ours knew we should meet and somehow we already did."

"They say out friends know us better than we know ourselves, maybe she knew something that we didn't."

"Maybe and maybe something so surreal is good thing."
"Surreal works for me, I think I've been looking for surreal for quite some time. I think I finally found it."
"Me too!"

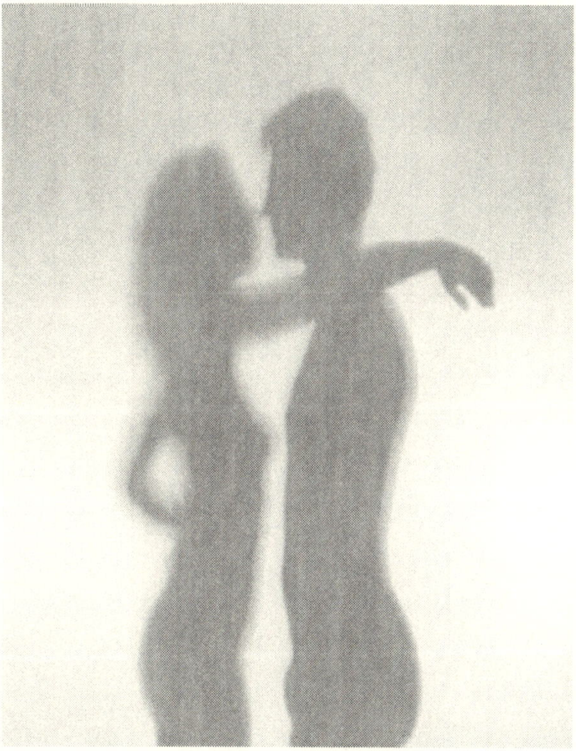

5

Richard, Mike, and Nicole

"Come on, can't you find something to wear already," Richard shouted to his roommate mike.

"Shut up man, finding the right shirt is just part of the process to impress the right woman," Mike said from his bedroom as he was looking through his closet for the right shirt to wear for their evening out. It was Friday night and Richard and Mike usually went out on the town trying to pick up women hoping that they would eventually find the right one that they could have a relationship with.

Mike was the type of guy that never knew what to wear- he had no fashion sense and was just as comfortable in an old pair of sweats and one of his favorite t-shirts as a pair of kakis and a nice button down shirt.

    Richard was already getting frustrated at his best friend so he decided to help him along and find the right shirt for him, which would be anything that he pulled out of the closet. Unlike his friend, he wasn't confused on the notion that you had to wear the right cloths to impress a woman; you only have to have a winning personality and be able to make them laugh to leave an impression on them. Richard walked in Mike's room and said. "Look just pick something out, I keep telling you that it doesn't matter what you wear-women like you for who you are despite being quite nerd-like. You are a great guy and can find a beautiful woman to go out with."

    Mike looked at his friend with a sarcastic look and replied. "Okay then how about this shirt," as he pulled out Star Wars shirt with a picture of Darth Vader on it.

    Richard gave him funny look and said, "well maybe not that shirt." You want to actually get a first date with someone and then on the fourth date you can let out your nerd side and see if they really like you."

"Hey you said any shirt and I don't care what anybody says, a Star Wars shirt is classy."

"Well I'm glad you don't care what anybody says because all they're going to say is you're a big nerd. Don't wear the shirt."

Mike put the shirt away and finally pulled out a nice polo shirt that looked like he could be playing in the Masters Golf tournament. He said, "In a perfect world I could find somebody that liked Sci-Fi just as much as me and we could a do a whole say of just watching Battlestar Galactica or Mystery Science Theater 3000. They got to be out there somewhere."

"There are-they're called men and you can usually find them at those conventions you like to go to all dressed up as their favorite character."

Mike started laughing because part of what Richard was saying that was true; it was mostly men that did like Sci-Fi and Fantasy, but he also knew that if he was lucky enough he just might meet somebody that shared that similar interest with him.

Finally, Richard and Mike left for the evening to take part in their usually barhopping ritual on a Friday night. When they turned old they made a pact that they would spend what free time they could going out and trying to find that special person that they could fall in love with instead of just sitting around hoping that she would appear or that they would find her online. Yes, they had tried that too, but all they met were the insane and the desperate and sometimes both. For Richard and Mike it was going out in public where women were hanging out or nothing at all, so they might actually have a chance of finding someone and not becoming that cute gay couple, which everybody was starting to believe they were. However, no matter where they went, they always ended up at The Matador.

∞∞∞∞∞

Richard and Mike had met in college when they were freshman and assigned to the same dorm room. Unlike some roommate situations in college that turned out weird their situation turned out to be the best thing for them. They became instant friends, best friends to be exact and it made college one of the best times in their lives. Even though they were not studying the same thing and never had classes together, they were rarely apart and they shared the same times of joy and the same heartbreaks.

Even though they shared some of the same similar interests, they were different people. Richard was more of the smooth, flirtatious type, which had no trouble talking with women. Mike on the other hand was shy and geek like which, never impressed any woman he met. He had a sarcastic personality though and in rare moments, he could be the life of the party and actually have women wanting to be with him. Only once though did he ever go home with a girl and get to spend the night with her; she was a teacher's aide who had a nerd like quality about her as well. For the most part women never seemed to be impressed and most of the time it was because he was smarter than them and never could relate to anyone outside of academics and who wants that in college.

Richard was different though, he never had a problem with getting laid and finding a girl to go home with. He never had any serious relationships in college and he was not to be tied down to just one woman. For him college was just an endless parade of panties and sex games, which for him winning was determined by how much he played. Someone had once told him that college was an endless orgy and he should take part in the experience because that was college. He did, quite literally and there were a few female professors of his that he played with during his college career.

    Richard and Mike eventually moved out of the dorm during college and they still remained roommates. When they both graduated and took jobs in Chicago never relocating somewhere else they decided to stay roommates until one of them decided to get married. They were best friends and even though both of them were on the lookout for that special someone, it wasn't something that they were going to find anytime soon. Being roommates was always fun throughout their twenties. And if nothing else because they could count on each other somehow the adventure together was always worth it. The way they looked at it, who needed a wife when they had a best friend. There was just one thing though, they were thirty years old now, with neat hair, and had lived together for 12 years so rumors began to surface. At this point, they had to wonder if they were gay, and then they would just watch some lesbian porn and be reminded that they really loved women.

    Living together in their spacious two-bedroom apartment three blocks from Wrigley field was never dull especially with Richard. The fact is his dating habits never changed while being out of college. Richard was as always the playboy bringing a variety of women home, while Mike remained the nerdy type who had problem finding the so-called meaningful relationship. He could get a date, but most dates never made it to two dates; the problem was he was himself every time and most women didn't understand him. Mike was a computer analyst, who read most things in the language of ones and zeros, he was a Science Fiction fan, and loved mythology. They were the things that never seemed to impress women, at least the women he met.

    Once a few years ago on his 26th birthday Mike finally did meet somewhat of a kindred spirit. She was fellow computer analyst, who had a flavor for Science Fiction combined with an awkward nerd like quality that Mike could only appreciate; more important she seemed to get Mike and he got her. They dated for about a year and a half until she was offered a job in Seattle; she moved away and wanted Mike to come with her, but he could never leave his home and she couldn't stay. As far as they were concerned it just wasn't meant to be. For Mike, it was the last time he ever had a serious relationship with someone and the older he got the more he thought to himself settling down was never going to happen. But the more he believed that the more he wanted to settle down.

Richard was different, he never wanted a serious relationship and in his mindset there were too many women that he could play around with instead of being annoyed by one for the rest of his life. So after college he continued to play around and was notorious for parading women in and out of his apartment. As he pursued his journalism career he was never short of finding some gal that he could flirt with, somebody that would excite him at least for a few moments, and that he could have fun with in the time frame of a night.

The problem was he had never met anyone that could challenge him or humble him. He never met anybody that could hold his level of conversation and make him look silly when he debated them. The one he was really looking for was the one that could baffle him, infuriate him, and could balance him with the same level of stubbornness. Even though he would only admit it on rare occasions, the woman that could do that was the woman he would spend the rest of his life with. So for now he just played around keeping himself from being bored. When asked by his friends to describe the type of women he wouldn't sleep with his answer was always men.

∞∞∞∞∞

    Richard and Mike started their evening at a few clubs that were known to be cool and filled with lots of beautiful and slutty women as Richard would point out to Mike. He was trying to get his friend laid knowing that Mike was in desperate need of female companionship. Mike was just trying to find someone that he could have a meaningful relationship with, he was looking for someone to talk with and to laugh with. Richard scoffed at that notion and according to his thinking a one-night stand could be just as satisfying or at least a break from the routine of a boring life.

Of course there were good-looking women at all the places they went to, but none of them seemed interested in Mike. Richard on the other hand flirted with everyone that he met collecting phone numbers for future one-night romps. Like every weekend they would eventually end up back at The Matador for sarcastic conversations and flirting with young college females who were never interested and just reminded Richard and Mike of how old they had become.

Richard and Mike took a seat at the bar and said hello to a few of the familiar faces that they knew. I walked up to them from behind the bar and got them their usual drinks. I said to them in a sarcastic tone. "You two out tonight looking for love."

"Don't say that evil word Trinidad" Richard replied back. "You can speak for Mike here, but I'm looking for the usual woman to share a bed with."

"What kind of woman is that," I asked.

"One with low standards...Of course an extra bonus would be if she's a 'hot."

"I'm glad to see you have some standards when it comes to finding woman to share your bed with."

"It's a moral issue, that's why you have to have standards, speaking of, there's a cute college girl sitting over there that's checking me out. I'll be right back."

Mike and I both started laughing at Richard as he walked away heading towards a table with a young girl who had piercing blues eyes. That just happened to be Richard's favorite thing. I looked at Mike and asked him "so how is the hunting going, meet anyone nice."

Mike let out a sarcastic life and said. "Yeah right, all I seem to meet are the alcoholic, depressed, slumming because my husband won't pay attention to me, so doped up on Prozac that they didn't even realize that I was a bit of a nerd. If they're somewhat normal they already figure out in the first five seconds of meeting me that I'm a loser."

"Well don't take it so hard there are a lot of stupid women out there and I don't think you're a loser. You're drink is on the house just show my appreciation for you."

"Isn't a free drink just a way of showing someone that you feel sorry for them?"

"Just enjoy your drink," I replied giving a sarcastic laugh.

Mike just smiled at my little joke for it was only a good friend that could insult you and make you feel better at the same time. Under any other circumstances it would have been just a patronizing bartender making fun of a customer while he took his money for a pathetic watered down drink. Richard spent the better part of twenty minutes talking the table full of college girls hoping that he could get at least one to go him with him even if it wasn't the one with blue eyes.

Mike just sat at the bar drinking alone watching the Cubs game on the TV enjoying his drink knowing full well that it would be the best part of the evening or he so he thought, What he and Richard didn't know was that night was the one that would their lives forever. They both would start a course in their lives that would change everything they believed and both would finally know why love was a sex game wrapped in a game of curiosity.

As Mike watched the ballgame he didn't take much notice at the people sitting at the bar around him. One in particular was a young woman who just happened to sit down next to him. She was stunning and simple; she was one who walked with a confidence of knowing who she was inside even if here nightlife was a façade. As she was sitting down next to Mike she tripped over herself and fell into Mike knocking him off his barstool, but in the process he did catch her and helped her back onto her feet. She apologized and sat down keeping her main focus on the ball game, which was the main reason she was sitting down at the bar while waiting for her friend.

    She got a drink and while watching the ballgame also realizing that Mike was engrossed in the same thing so she decided to start a conversation with him even though she never did that in a bar. She looked at Mike giving him a small serene smile and said. "I'm sorry for knocking into you, I know I already apologized before, but I just wanted to say it again and thank you again for being so nice. Despite looking beautiful and graceful, I'm quite the klutz." She was trying to be sarcastic and witty in order to make him laugh, and it worked.

    Mike laughed at her comments and replied. "I know what you mean, I don't look like I can move gracefully, but I have a few cool moves that impress people like I just demonstrated when catching you. Although you don't have to apologize again, it was no problem what so ever to help you."

"Well I just didn't want you thinking I couldn't appreciate a nice guy like you and that was a really cool move."

Mike smiled at her and for the rest of the evening they ignored the ballgame and started talking to each other. It was a nice to change for Mike, she was beautiful and he could already tell she had a bit of a goofy side. So they started off by introducing themselves and for the first time in a few years a woman looked at him directly in the eyes and introduced herself, her name was Nicole.

Nicole was a few years younger than Mike and she was a nursing student. A few years back she had decided that her other career was not really working out for her and she needed a change. She still did her old job on the side just to make extra money and to help put herself through school. She really wanted a career where she could help people by letting out her compassionate side instead of a job that had its less than reputable means and could be a little dangerous. So she decided to go back to school and become a registered nurse.

She had a few friends, but with her schedule she never really got to go out much and when she did it was mostly alone at a familiar place watching a ballgame. The Matador was one her favorite places just because of the good imported beer and lively conversation from me and my wife, which she hadn't gotten to known over the last few years. She was a big baseball fan, the only good thing that she got out from her alcoholic father; she never got anything from her junkie mother who was found dead in an alley somewhere after she had overdosed on cocaine when Nicole was only three. Part of the reason she wanted to become a nurse was to help people like that before it was too late.

Nicole and Mike started their conversation off by talking about baseball. Mike asked her. "So you must be a big Cubs fan if you're in here alone watching the ball game."

"Yeah, I admit I love baseball and the Cubs are a little bit of a passion for me."

"Well I don't care what anyone says that definitely makes you hot. We as men are always looking for a woman that likes sports just as much as us."

"It's even worse. I'm a Science Fiction Fan. For some reason I just loved it as a kid and still do."

Mike laughed a little bit and replied to her. "Now you're just a nerd, it's not really attractive either."

Nicole didn't know if he was serious because Mike being sarcastic sounded just like if he was serious. She said to him in a serious manner. "Do you really think so, I always thought I was kind of pretty."

"I was kidding," he replied. "Being a Science Fiction Fan is not a bad thing. I think it's kind of cool mainly because I'm one. You also have nothing to worry about when it comes being pretty, your gorgeous just in case you were wondering. "

Nicole smiled at him and replied back. "I was hoping you would say that. You got a very serious tone to your sarcasm."

"It's my way of be condescending and nice all at the same time so I can make fun of stupid people."

"You think I'm a stupid person?"
"No."
"I don't know If I believe you."

He looked at her and looked at all her features and then replied back. "Look at my face and tell me if I'm lying to you," letting out a smile in the process.

She looked at him and after a brief pause said. "You are sincere. I can tell"

"I never lie about a beautiful woman."

"I guess you wouldn't lie about something like that, at least that's my first impression."

"I'm a guy who's not had a date in long time so there would be no reason for me to lie. Besides I'm not that great at it anyway."

"I guess Science Fiction people never get any breaks."

"You're right and that's a shame because we are usually really smart people, but you're really hot so I don't think you would have any problems."

Nicole smiled at Mike for his graceful sincerity while being witty and clever. She said to Mike. "I think you should get a break because you a really nice guy, someone that knows how to properly treat a woman."

"What makes you think that I'm really that nice?"

"Because you first response to me was not some cheap sexist pick up line about how I would look good in your bed. You actually started talking to me like good people do when they want to get to know somebody."

Mike laughed because she was seeing the type of guy he really was and he didn't have to hide the fact that he may not be the best looking and that he was nerdy. The thing is she didn't mind all that; she was interested in him, in who he really was. Mike was excited not that a beautiful woman was talking to him, but that she liked him for being himself, but more importantly she could be herself without the façade of being a beautiful woman. And that's how it started with Nicole and Mike. They sat there for the rest of the evening talking about life while ignoring everything around them as if they were the only two people alive. Nicole and Mike were like those two lost souls who had been wondering alone for so long until they finally meet.

After awhile when the connection between them was strong Nicole invited Mike back to her place to watch a movie, it was a sci-fi movie and one that she knew he would appreciate especially not knowing the truth about her and her not wanting to admit it herself. The move they watched just happened to be Blade Runner, a favorite for both of them.

While Mike and Nicole disappeared to her place, Richard stayed behind talking with Paula most of the night. When he was with her he forgot about all the young college girls that he could flirt with. Paula, even though a bit annoying in her feisty sarcastic attitude was still more interesting than some young hussy that didn't know anything about the real world yet. Maybe that's why he chose to talk to her instead of the young girls in the bar. Even though he would never admit it, he liked talking to her and she liked talking to him because they kept each other on their toes.

Richard looked at her with his sarcastic smile and asked her. "So while you've been doing the lawyer thing the last five years, did you get married?"

She replied satirically. "You didn't see a ring on my ginger did you?"

"No, but that doesn't mean anything. I've met a lot married women that don't like wearing their wedding ring."

"While out on one of your sex romps, no doubt."

"Hey, I meet people all the time because I'm a journalist. It's not necessarily something sexual when I meet these women."

"It is most of the time and you know how I know that because you still walk into a room and look for all the young girls too stupid to know what you're talking about or the bored housewife that needs somebody to make her feel pretty even if it's just for a night."

    Richard laughed at her comment, not because it was that funny, but because she knew him that well. Paula and Richard had a history together and fact was, Richard was still the same playboy that he was in college. She knew that because he acted the same and still remembered the night they spent together once in college. She foolishly thought back then that she would be different and it could be the start of something, but it never was. He forgot about her and continued to sleep with every woman he met or at least try to. Paula did have a crush on him back then because he was good looking with that All American smile and was somebody that could make anybody laugh and feel good about themselves even without remembering their name. After that night when he never remembered her she just went back to despising him.

    Truth was he did like her then and still liked her now, but sometimes we never get out of that immature stage where the honesty escapes us. He finally asked her what he really wanted to know, "so are you dating someone?"

"No, why are asking me that. You want to ask me out or something?"

"No. I just want to make sure that a big jealous guy doesn't pop out of the corner and try to kick my ass."

"You don't have anything to worry about. I'm not dating anyone. I'd ask you, but that would be a silly question."

"Dating is not a word I use. If you use that term then it might lead to something."

"I know that would be bad because you would have to remember her name and that might be too complicated with you."

Richard couldn't help but laugh at her sarcasm, it was one of the most attractive things about her. The normal things like stubbornness and sarcastic commentary would be a big turn off for people, but they were the very things that attracted them to one another. It was the reason they could still talk to each other ten years later and never have those awkward moments that people have between them when they can't be honest with each other. Now for Richard and Paula they weren't quite there yet, but they were on their way through their only way of communication, sarcasm and insults. It's the perfect way to start out be for men and women because in learning how to infuriate one another you find what makes you never want to be away from each other. For the rest of the evening until the bar closed Paula and Richard just kept talking and swapping bad date stories

Somewhere through the course of their conversation Paula and Richard agreed to meet for dinner the next night. Neither one of them could say for sure why they were going on a date because they still couldn't figure out why they liked each other, or at least they couldn't admit it yet. That night was also the first time in long time that Richard had gone home alone. When he got there at midnight he found that his roommate wasn't there and he smiled at the fact that Mike might have actually gotten lucky that night.

The next day Richard was up somewhat early-before 10 am. He started making coffee and as he started to drink his first cup he was greeted by his roommate walking through the door. Richard just smiled at him and asked him. "So this is a nice change, me getting coffee and you walking through the door, did you actually get some last night."

Mike tried to be serious and a gentleman all at the same time by not saying anything at first. Finally, a minute or so had passed and with Richards's curiosity looming over him he replied with a big smile. "Okay fine, yes I did and it was awesome."

"Dude you are officially my hero this morning," Richard replied.

"As well I should be because not only did I have sex last night, she was fucking hot."

"What was she on the scale?"

"Looks-a nine. Intelligence- a nine. And personality without the insanity-a nine."

"No way, hey if she can cook and has no terminal illness, you should marry her."

"Who knows, all I can say she was beautiful, clever, and she had great taste in movies. Last night we went back to her place and watched Blade Runner."

"No way, now I know you're lying about her."

"I couldn't believe it either, she's a Science Fiction Fan. I even gave her the test."

"You ask her if she liked Star Wars and told her that you were a Star Wars geek…you can't do that on a first date. It violates the first date rules. Even if she was 100 percent fantastic you have to wait till the third date before giving her the test."

"You're right and it makes sense to do that, but I was so enamored with her I wanted to bypass that because I may not get a third date much less a second one. Meeting her last night could just be a fluke or a one of the planets out of alignment."

Richard smiled and replied. "That's true and I understand that logic, but you made a mistake that a man who hasn't had sex in a long time tends to make. When the little guy stands up to say hi you let him do the thinking, only if she's naked on the bed ready for you to take advantage. Any other scenario will get you into trouble and it usually costs you money. "

Mike nodded in agreement and hung his head down knowing that he had made a mistake under the man's code of ethics for dating. He looked at Richard and in a serious tone replied. "I might have made a mistake, but I haven't told you the outcome of the test."

"Okay what happened?"

" I came home this morning what do you think?"

"Wait you gave her the test before you had sex with her and you still passed?"

Mike nodded yes and started to smile. Richard gave him a surprised look and didn't know what to say to him, he was still shocked as he continued to drink his coffee. Finally Mike look at him after a few moments and replied. "You know you want to say it."

Richard shook his head no and Mike said. "Say it or the next girl you bring over I'll tell her that you're the Star Wars nerd."

Richard said. "Alright fine, you're the man."

"Who's the man?"

"You're the man."

Mike started laughing as he poured himself a cup of coffee. Richard looked at him and had to ask. "How did you get away with giving her the test and still getting to have sex with her? Wait I know how this happened, the girl you went home with had a sister in coma and that's who you slept with."

Mike gave him a dirty look for his horrible suggestion. Richard responded again "Or maybe she was bipolar with a fringe of multiple personalities and her real self doesn't know you."

Mike gave him a dirty look again and then replied. "No matter what strange scenario you come up with it'll be wrong, Nicole was completely sane, she was hot and she liked me for me."

'Nicole...well at least she has a normal name. I still think there's something crazy about her. Then again even ugly people get a little luck from time to time of course that kind of thing only happens when you get the first three minutes free to a $3.99 phone call."

"Say what you want, but this is more than luck, I think God has seen fit to bless this humble soul. At this point in my life I more than deserve it unlike you. Speaking of, is the girl you brought home last night already up and gone or is she still sleeping?"

Richard laughed to himself about the strange twist of fate, Mike gets to go home with a hot girl and he slept alone for the first time in a long time. He said. "If you must know, I spent the evening talking with Paula and came home alone."

"Paula from college, I thought you two hated each other."

"Well, we do, somewhat. But I had a lot fun talking with her last night and I still get a kick out of tormenting her."

As he finished his sentence Mike's cell phone started ringing. He got excited thinking it was Nicole so he answered it without looking at the caller ID.

The person on the other end told him it was Rachel's Service and that she had a date for Nicole at 7:00 pm. Mike tried to tell her that she had the wrong number then he heard the other voice say the name Nicole so he inquired about the people calling instead of just hanging up the phone. The voice asked him who he was and then after he said his name was Mike the voice replied that they were Rachel's escort service.

Mike had to ask again to confirm that what he heard was true. The voice told him again that they were Rachel's Escort Service and that they were looking for Nicole to tell her that she had a date that night. Mike didn't know what to say, but he did say again to the woman on the phone that she had the wrong number or that he had the wrong phone. The voice just told Mike if he saw Nicole again to tell her to check in because she had a date at 7:00 pm.

Mike sat down in shock and Richard asked him. "What's wrong, who was on the phone?"

"It was an escort service looking for Nicole to tell her that she had a date to night. Apparently Nicole is a hooker."

"How do you know for sure maybe it's really a wrong number and they're just looking for someone named Nicole."

Mike looked at the phone which looked exactly like his and then he checked the settings to see if it was his, it wasn't because the background image wasn't Star Wars like on his phone. He looked up at Richard and said. "It's not my phone, it's hers. It looks like she has the same exact phone as mine."

"Are you sure?'

"No Star Wars background, as long as I have had a cell phone I have always had a Star Wars background. I never wanted anything else."

Richard gave Mike a look of general concern and started to laugh. He wasn't making fun of his friend, but he was laughing at the situation. It was bad luck for Mike, but it was funny in a way even if Mike couldn't see it yet. Richard replied to his friend. "Sorry buddy, that sucks, but it's kind of funny."

"How is this funny, I meet a great girl who I actually have something in common with and she turns out to be a whore. Hell, how do I even know if I had something in common with her; it could have just been an act with her so she could eventually get money out of me? Then again it could be a scam."

Richard patted his friend on the shoulder and said. "Calm down, if she wanted money then she would have required you to leave it on the dresser. As for a scam she didn't scam you. Do you realize what godlike thing you just did, you slept with a hooker without paying her money or coke. How many guys can actually say that? Face it dude you're a hero to every man in the world."

Mike looked at his friend with a dirty look and replied. "Is that supposed to make me feel better?'

"I'm just saying it could be worse- you did wear a condemn didn't you?

"I may be a little stupid after sleeping with a call girl, but I'm not that stupid."

Richard laughed at his friend's remarks and then he went to pour himself another cup of coffee. He replied back. "I know you're not that stupid, not wearing a condemn is something I would do and I've been through enough pregnancy scares to know better. The only thing I can hope for is that I do have a low sperm count. You know you're doing pretty bad when you pray for low sperm to get past your own stupidity."

Mike finally laughed at his friends remarks. Richard always had an uncanny way of making people laugh when they needed it the most. He got up and grabbed his car keys and then started for the door. Richard asked him where he was going and all Mike could say was that he had to talk to her and get the whole damn truth.

About thirty minutes later he arrived back at Nicole's place. After his persistent knocking she answered the door with a smile. He tried to smile back, but couldn't get one out. She asked him. "Are you okay, normally when somebody spend the night with someone they had a good time with they're not unhappy to return."

Mike asked her. "Is that before or after they leave the money?"

She stared at him with a dumbfounded look not knowing how to respond to his comment. Mike looked waiting for a response, but she didn't have one. Finally he said to her. "I have your phone and you have mine. I got a call from Rachel's about an hour ago."

She finally had a horrified look on her face realizing what he knew now. She tried to say something in her defense, but

Mike cut her off before she could say anything. He said. "Please tell me it's not true, you're not a call girl are you?"

She replaced her horrified look with a serious one and said "It's true I am a call girl and I work through a service."

"I imagine you are a very high priced call girl."

"Very. More than you can afford. Does that make you feel better?"

"Not really, but I am curious about something? "

"How I can be a call girl and why did I invite you home last night without telling you or charging you?" Nicole said this to Mike before he could ask his own question.

"Yeah, something like that!"

Nicole took a seat on her couch and tried to figure out the best way to explain this in a way that he might understand. She said to him "You have to understand something I didn't get into this work lightly and I was beaten as a child or molested, and it really isn't as bad as you think. I pick who I go out with and never do anything that puts my health or life in jeopardy."

Mike asked her. "Do men pay you for sex?"

"Yes they do?"

"Then it's exactly what I think it is and yes it sounds bad?"

"I know it does and there is nothing I can say that will change that, but know one thing. I was a girl who liked a guy for who he was and brought him home just to be with him. I didn't do it for money."

"Not good enough because what it really amounts to is can you quit your day job for that guy?"

"I do this to pay for school and I'm almost done. I went back to school because I don't want to do this anymore."

"It's understandable, but I don't know how to deal with this."

After that Mike got up to leave. Nicole said to him as he was walking out the door "I want to see you again and not as a client. I want to be with you because I like you." Mike turned around to say something, but nothing came out so he just walked away not looking back to see the sad look upon her face.

Mike didn't go home right away. He had some thinking to do; he wanted to figure out how God could give him something wonderful and then take it away with a disgusting lie. No matter how much fun he had with Nicole or how great she really was he couldn't get past her being an escort.

The truth was Nicole was as normal as you and I or anybody you would meet in a bar. There was nothing about her to suggest that she could be a prostitute. She came from a normal middle class family and although she had somewhat of a broken home it wasn't any worse than anybody else that she had grown up with.

Her mother and father divorced when she was ten. She lived with her mother until she died in a car crash when Nicole was thirteen and then lived with her father until she graduated High School at the age of seventeen. She was close to both her parents and even though her parents could never make their marriage work, they never used Nicole to get back at each other. When it came to her they were both loving parents right up to the day that her mother died.

Nicole was normal in every way growing up. She had her bouts of rebellion, experimented with drugs and sex when she was a teenager, and she even ran away once or twice for only a few days before she would return home knowing that being with her father was better than life on the streets. She was close to her father and he was a good man for the most part even though he was a hard man when it came to her, he was always involved and very protective when it came to her well being until his accidental death when she was nineteen.

Nicole was in her second year of community college when her father was hot by a drunk driver and was killed instantly. It was crushing and a burden she had to carry because she didn't have any family left. She went her period of grieving and even dropped out of school for a while and that's when it began for her. She had to go through her rebellion against life; she had to take that treacherous path into the abyss so she could find the voice of salvation.

Even though there was nothing in her childhood that would cause her to make such horrific choices there was tragedy that slowly devoured her soul to where she didn't know who she was anymore. One night at a party with some friends when she was high on a dose of heroin, she was somehow convinced to prostitute herself to the dealer in order to score more drugs. She was so high that night that she never even realized what she did - in front and behind and in a place that she had never dared to go before.

That's how it started with her; one night, a rush with a serious kick, and a high to which she had never experienced before. Nicole was hooked and developed a small drug habit and with not much money to spare she had to pay for it with small favors and there were many men that took payment. Nicole went through this for about two years before a friend got her clean and told her that if she was going to be a whore she might as well get paid for it and not in small amounts. Her friend Mary that she had grown up in taught her how to be a high-class escort making lots of money.

    Considering that she had been at the bottom of the abyss being an escort was something she didn't seem to mind. Nicole even liked it to a degree because even though it was prostitution she was in control. She never slept with anybody that she didn't want to and she set the price. She made lots of money and it was really good money after she kicked her drug habit; it was the right amount of money for a new life and chance to start over when the life didn't interest her anymore. Nicole was perfect example of when we fall, we fall hard and after we find the voice of salvation at the bottom of the abyss it's only inch-by-inch that we crawl our way back. She had been there at the bottom a few times before and she was getting out the only she knew how, slowly, one day at a time, one nursing class at a time.

Eventually Mike ended up back at his place with supplies-he had been to the liquor store. Richard gave him a funny look as he walked through the door with two big bags of booze. He said. "So I guess it didn't go well."

"No," Mike replied.

"I see you have lots of booze, is it going to be one of those days?"

"I think so."

"Alright then! So are you never going to see her again?"

"I guess not."

"Just making sure you got it out of your system – you never let go of things very easily."

Mike poured himself a tall glass of 21-year-old scotch- he wasn't fucking around that night in trying to forget. After a few drinks between Richard and Mike while on a good route to being drunk by the afternoon Mike began to talk about what happened between him and Nicole.

He said. "I can't believe she's and escort and she didn't even try to lie to me."

"I guess that's something." Richard replied back as they sat at their kitchen table drinking their liquor straight.

"I mean she was cool, she was classy, and of course that could be just part of the act. She had a great sense of humor. Most important I got to watch Blade Runner with her, how many chicks do you ever get to do that with?"

"A hot girl and a great Sci-Fi movie- doesn't happen often. It's a once in a lifetime opportunity when it comes to being happy."

Mike gave him a surprised look and said. "You're right it is a once in a life time opportunity and we're only talking about one minor annoyance that will eventually disappear."

"Oh God," Richard said with a concerned tone. "You want to see her again...you know you can't right?"

"Why not?"

"She's a hooker and eventually she'll have to charge you."

"I don't think it's that big of deal, shocking yes, but I can learn to deal with it and it's not like she can be one forever."

"You are going to try and reform her, aren't you?"

Mike poured himself another drink and replied. "She's already reforming herself, why can't I be her friend and help her. Damn the morality behind being a hooker."

Richard paused for a moment and with serious tone said. "I understand where you're coming from, you meet this great girl who you might be able to have a life with, but she will always have the hooker thing hanging around her neck-do you think good can really come from that?"

"Maybe, I don't know for sure, but I want to find out."

"Okay, fine, but before you do see what's out there first. Really take a look this time and see if you can't find a great girl that's not into sexual deviancy."

"What do you suggest?"

"Let's do some serial dating and really try the online thing-it might actually work if you give a 110% to it. For example that Net Harmony might actually be a good one-they say you're forced to tell the truth about yourself with the all the questions you have to answer to make your profile."

Mike gave him a sarcastic look and replied. "Right, there is no possible way one can lie on the internet."

"Just try it and see what happens."

"What if I don't want to?"

"You can never know for sure if this Nicole girl is the right one for you without taking a chance and seeing what else is out there."

"You know that really doesn't make sense."

Richard gave Mike a dirty look and said. "I don't care, we are going to do this because I don't want you pining over a hooker, who I'm sure will screw you over in the end-no pun intended."

"Fine I will humor you, but if this turns out to be a disaster you can't say shit about Nicole and you have to let me be when it comes to dating."

"Alright then."

"You know you shouldn't say anything to begin with all the women you parade in and out of here. You're just as a bad as a hooker. The only difference between you and Nicole is she gets paid for it and she probably makes more money than you do."

Richard laughed at his friend's remarks and replied. "If I could get away with charging women for the privilege of getting to have sex with me I would. But there are only so many times you can role-play the hooker scenario. I mean that one girl that liked to play the game of rape is one in a million, I've never met anyone like her, but she was cool in her own way."

Mike and Richard laughed while finishing the first bottle of scotch. For the rest of the day they drank liquor and put there profiles on some of the online dating sites. By the end of the day they were so hammered that they didn't have a clue of what they putting in their profile. They were on a quest to see who they could find to make them forget their wretched and painful love lives. They were going to keep dating until they found somebody for the both of them. No matter what it took and no matter what crazy scenario they came up with to meet women they made a pact to keep searching. What they hadn't figured out yet was they had already found those people, but didn't know what to do about it, they were too busy convincing themselves of the lie they created to find happiness.

    Richard and Mike had their profiles on three or four sites and they had some luck with it. For the next two months they each had two or three dates a week. None of them really went past two dates and for different reasons. Richard was only interested in sleeping with the women he met. Sometimes he succeeded and sometimes the woman would make up some crappy excuse to cut the evening short. Mike on the other hand really tried to get to know the women he went out with, but things never changed with him. The women he went out with never got him and were uninterested very quickly. He always thought to himself, it was the story of his life.

Richard and Mike tried just about everything to meet women, online dating, meeting random women at the bar, and even speed dating. However, it never amounted to anything for the both of them. Mike wanted to see Nicole again because despite what she did for a living, he still liked her. Richard would sleep with his date the first time they went out and never call them again or if the date went sour he would end up buying dinner for Paula and bringing it to her at work because she was always working late.

After a couple of months of the whole dating situation Richard and Mike were still where they were two months before when it came to finding love. So much so that both of them were even going out with the women that they weren't that interested in to begin with. One night when Mike was checking his account on the Net Harmony website he saw another email from the woman that had started corresponding with him a month earlier even though he just ignored it because he wasn't interested in her based on her profile. Mike asked Richard what he should do and after looking the profile Richard simply told him to take a chance. He also told Mike that because she looked like a kinky person it might be good for him since he had not been laid in a while.

  Mike gave Richard his usual dirty look when he said something crass, but in a way he knew his friend was right. Richard would go on to tell him that like every woman he met had to take a chance no matter what so why should this be any different. Besides, you never know what you might get with a woman and sometimes it could actually be good. Mike decided to take a chance and so he emailed her. He had a date with her the next night.

  Richard also had one with some girl he met online; she was a kindergarten teacher and as he would later find out after a few dates, she would turn out to be a restraining order waiting to happen. She would call him thirty times in an hour wanting to know when she was going to see him again and all Richard could think about in the end was there was a mental hospital waiting to collect her. She was also a Baptist and Richard thought, maybe that had something to do with it.

The next night both Richard and Mike left on their dates. Mike found out that the girl who had been emailing him was actually kind of cool and somebody if given the opportunity on the first date would have sex with him. Mike thought that was great and decided to take the chance with her.

Eventually after dinner Mike and his date ended up back at her place so they could watch a movie or not watch a movie and just make out, which might lead to something else.

Richard was done with his date fairly early, a couple of hours to be a exact. The kindergarten teacher was really in to him and after a quick meal they ended up back at her place having sex a couple of times before Richard made up some excuse about work so he could leave. For Richard it was only about sex and whether the girl wanted to admit it or not, she needed somebody to make her feel good in an intimate way. Like most women that confuse sex and love as if they were the same thing and have the same emotional attachments she masqueraded her feelings for Richard with the notion that she really wanted a relationship with him. Richard was smart enough to know better for he had been playing women for years to keep from being bored with them and he was already bored with the kindergarten teacher.

Richard left her place and decided to grab some dinner for him and Paula because he knew she would be working late again as usual and could use some company. He arrived at her law firm and walked in saying hello to the security man who he was already on a first name basis with because the security man just assumed like everybody who worked there that Richard was Paula's boyfriend. Paula saw Richard walking to her office with good Chicago Style sandwiches, her favorite. She said to him as he walked up. "Are you readying my mind tonight or something, you just knew that I'd be hungry right about now."

Richard replied. "I could tell you yes and try to make you thing that I'm actually a mind reader, but that only works on 19 year old Psych students who don't know any better. Besides I'm not dumb enough to lie to a lawyer."

"You're just dumb in other areas aren't you?"

"Aren't all men like that to a degree."

"You don't want me to answer that honestly?"

Richard handed her a sandwich and a beer then she gave him a hug for the dinner. It was beginning to be a ritual with them. Since she worked long hours, sometimes until ten at night skipping dinner in the process, he would bring her food about three nights a week and on Friday night's they would go out and have a drink. They didn't realize it yet, but they were dating. They talked to each other more than they talked to most people. Most of the time it was arguing, but in a playful way. The thing was they just liked to talk to each other and even though they could not admit it yet talking to each other was the best part of both their days.

Paula asked Richard. "So what are you up tonight?"

Richard replied. "Oh the usual, it was a hard day of writing about Chicago Sports-the Cubs won by the way." Paula just shook her head at Richard and kind of rolled her eyes at him-she thought it was funny that even though Richard knew she wasn't a baseball fan he would still tell her what was going on with the Cubs anyway. Richard continued what her was saying. "The only other thing that happened with me was that I had a date that really didn't last too long."

"You had a date tonight and you still ended up at my office having dinner with me. I don't know whether to be mad or feel sorry for you that it didn't work out."

"The date was short, but that doesn't mean it didn't work out."

"You couldn't have slept with her already."

"Oh no I slept with her-how long do you think it takes to have a sex a few times before you're done and you can leave?"

Paula just gave him a dirty look and paused for a moment. Richard asked her what was wrong and she replied. "This is why you're a pig and why we never got a long in college."

Richard shook his head in disbelief at her comments and asked her. "What are you so mad about its not like I took advantage of you, I didn't even do anything to her."

"Yes you did – does she realize that you're in it for the sex and nothing else?"

"If she doesn't know then she'll figure it out. I'm not lying to her."

"You're not telling her the real truth ...silence doesn't always mean you're telling the truth, silence can sometimes mean a lack of honesty."

Richard laughed at Paula's comments as she gave him a dirty look. Richard could never understand that when it came to women when you screw one over, you screw the entire gender over-it was just something a man never understood. He replied. "You should look at this as a compliment –I could still be with her, but I wanted to see you instead. You're much more beautiful and exciting."

Paula continued to give him a dirty look and replied back "You can try all you want, but I deal with bullshit all day and I work in an office with mostly men so there is a lot of it here. There is nothing you can say that I can't read between the lines and figure out what you're really trying to say."

"Is it the job of a lawyer to be cynical all the time and constantly think what is being said to them is bullshit?"

"I get paid lots of money to be this way."

Richard just laughed because no matter how much they might be mad at each other they always had a way of making each other laugh with their playful banter back and forth. Paula finally asked. "So how come you have been on so many dates lately?"

Richard laughed and said. "I told you before I'm helping Mike go through the dating process so he can actually find someone nice and without any major hang-ups."

"Right because he went out with the call girl, but why are you going on these dates when you have no intentions of trying to be serious with any one of them."

"I could lie and say it's just to help Mike, but I don't need to date in order to do that. Really, it's just the sex."

"At least you're honest. Although, you realize how much of a scoundrel you are by lying to these women and using them for sex."

"It's not entirely for that – someday it's going to make a great story and I'll write about it."

"Oh, now I get it. This is all for research."

"Sure, part of it is."

"Am I part of that research?"

"No, I actually like you – this is the fun part of my day."

"You're a jackass, you know it. One of the girls you seduce and screw over all in the name of research is going to be such a wreck emotionally that you will push her over the edge until she's living in a hospital or dead."

Richard smirked at her remarks and replied. "If she's that volatile emotionally she doesn't need to be dating or have any kind of human contact where she runs the risk of being hurt. She's just being stupid if she does."

"Sometimes I really hate talking to you – you're a real jackass, you know."

"That much we know is true."

As Paula and Richard started laughing his cell phone rang with a call from the police, it was about Mike and there had been an accident. Richard was his emergency contact and since Richard knew most of the police officers in that area Mike thought that by calling him certain discretion could be kept over what happened to him. However, a journalist never has discretion as long as it's good for print. Richard told Paula that he had to go for there had been an incident with Mike. He kissed her goodbye and left.

About thirty minutes later Richard showed up at an apartment complex to a scene of police cars and an ambulance. Mike was being checked out by the paramedics and the police officers were taking statements from the neighbors. As Richard walked over to where the officers were he walked past a police car with a woman handcuffed in the backseat lying face down and passed out. He thought it was strange and then started to realize that Mike had been attacked. The lead officer walked over to Richard who he had known for some years now and began to tell the tale of Mike's incident.

It was Mike's date that had caused the incident-she attacked him and it was more than just slapping him a few times out of anger. She hit him hard with her fists and tore his cloths as he tried to get away. Mike was not the type of guy to just hit a woman even when defending himself so he did the next best thing, he tried to get away and keep her at bay with a broom.

The officer explained to Richard that the domestic disturbance started while they were watching a movie and in the middle of an argument Mike had made a comment about her being a bitch. It's a serious no, no with guys even though the statement might be true at times. It still wasn't a good cause for the violent outburst by the woman, but it's what triggered her insanity. It was that and the fact that she was a drug addict. That night she had taken a couple hits of speed, which lead to her anger erupting like a volcano.

After the police officer explained all the details to Richard including the part where the woman tried to grab the officer's gun and then had to be put unconscious by being shot with a tranquilizer Richard started laughing. He thought the part about being put down with tranquilizers was especially funny. Richard couldn't stop laughing because it was like a C.OP.S. episode on TV where none of the criminals seemed to have shirts on and they were the definition of trailer trash. The people on that show never seemed to know why they were being arrested even though a few pounds of cocaine were found on their coffee table inside their trailer.

Richard walked over to where Mike was sitting in the ambulance being checked out by the paramedics. He passed by the squad car and looked in the back seat seeing the woman handcuffed and passed out in the back again. He smiled again at the situation because no matter how horrible it might be it was still funny. He walked up to Mike and asked him. "So how was your date?"

"Fuck you," Mike replied.

"Well, I see you're still in shock."

"Shock, how about anger you fucking bastard. She tried to stab me."

"I know you're angry and you every right to be, but you got to admit this is kind of funny."

"Funny, I officially have the worst date story now."

"And it's something to brag about, even worth of a free drink."

Mike didn't laugh at his comments; he couldn't see the humor in this yet even though it was funny. All Mike could see was that it was a reminder of how you never know what you'll get on the internet and no matter what people will pretty much lie about themselves on a dating site. Mike was still too mad at Richard for listening to him in the first place about going on a date with that woman. He knew she was crazy, but he had to listen to Richard and as it turned out he should have listened to his own instinct.

Mike replied to his friend before he punched him. "I'm not interested in a free drink, I just want to find a girl I can laugh with and the sex is fantastic. I certainly don't want somebody that's going to put me in the hospital. To find that means I can't listen to you anymore." Then he punched Richard – hard enough to make fall to the ground.

As Richard fell down from his friend punching him in the face he shouted. "You don't have to hit me to stop listening me."

"I know, but it felt good."

Later that night Richard and Mike got drunk and laughed at the whole thing as best friends tend to do in the end. That same night Mike deleted whatever profiles he had on dating websites-he was done and for first time he knew who he wanted to be with no matter how complicated it would be. Richard on the other hand just went back to doing what he always did, except for one added wrinkle to his routine. Whenever he was done with whatever date he had with some young college or grad student that was impressed with him because he was an experienced journalist he would without fail end up seeing or talking to Paula. She had become the last and most important person he talked to at the end of the day- for some reason it just made sense as they became great friends.

They were spending most of their free time together and they had become a part of each other's lives. So as this came to be it became no surprise that one night when they were having dinner in her office late one night he leaned in and kissed her.

It wasn't the same friendly kiss that they had before, but something more affectionate and stronger in passion. She didn't turn away from it, but instead embraced it for she had wanted just as much as he did. After months of being with each other and becoming best friends their relationship became something more. They became a couple and Richard stopped sleeping around with different women. For the first time in his life he just wanted to be with one woman and he quickly figured out that it was the best thing he could have ever found.

      A few days after the worst date of his life Mike made a decision. He wasn't going to listen to the standards of society or what his friends and family might say. He knew who he wanted to be with; he knew who made him feel good. So after he got off work on the following Monday he didn't go straight home; he showed up at Nicole's place. He paused for a moment before knocking thinking again about what he was doing. He knocked on her door and she happened to be home.

      She answered the door and didn't say anything waiting for Mike to say something first. All he could say was, "I was wrong to get so mad. I shouldn't have walked out."

"Are you here for pleasure or business?"

"What do you mean?"

"If you're here for business with a call girl then I'm not open for business."

"I'm not here for that. I came to see you, I came to see the girl I met in the bar and I don't care about your occupation."

Nicole gave him a surprised look and replied back. "Is that really true or are you just saying that in the hope that I might still like you."

"I don't care. It does bother me, but I think you're still the same person that I met that night and had a great time with."

"I haven't changed and I'm not proud of what I do, but it's the only way I can support myself right now so I can finish nursing school. Still I'm not interested in anybody that's trying to change me."

Mike looked at her and paused before saying anything. He smiled a half smile trying to sympathize with her in some way and then he said. "I don't want to change you because I actually like who you are, but I don't have to like what you do."

"And you don't get to say anything about it. My occupation is off limits in our conversations. You don't get to lecture me or try to change me."

"That's the second time you've said that and I got it the first time."

"I only repeat myself because the few guys that found out immediately tried to change me...tried to make me into something that I'm not."

"I'm only interested in you and changing you would be something that I would end up disliking so what's the point."

Nicole let him come inside so they could finish talking. She asked him as he walked inside. "What about if we go out in public or we hang out with your friends- are you going to be embarrassed to be seen with me?'

"No."

"Are you going to tell anybody what I am?"

"No because it's nobody's business. But there are people that I can't tell because they won't understand."

"So you are embarrassed of me?"

"No, but I can't tell certain people just like you can't tell people that know what you are about me."

"Then what's the point when it comes to honesty- you've got to have that if a relationship is going to work.."

Mike gave her a very serious look and sighed. He then replied to her. "It doesn't work that way because of other people, not us. It's just the way it is. People that we know, that we're associated with wouldn't understand, but I've decided to be your friend and I've decided I want to be with you."

"What if I don't like the conditions of this friendship?"

"Then you don't have to be a part of it, but do you really want that?"

Nicole looked at him and smiled. She knew he made a good point. She said to him "I guess we're stuck in one hell of situation then."

"Yes we are, but I guess it only matter's what we think and of course what we want to do with this."

She smiled and said. "I guess we're going to find out how this works. I'm game if you are."

"So am I."

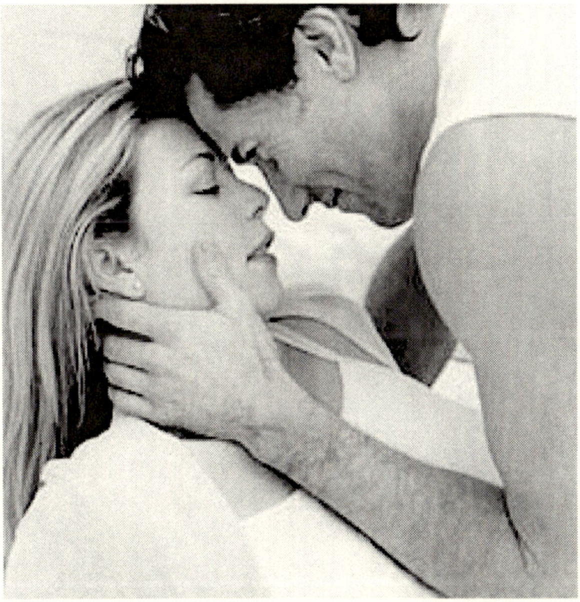

6

When All Hell Breaks Loose

So it finally happened; the players had their partners. Each of them had found someone that they could be with even if it was a kindred spirit in misery. Things were actually starting to look up for all of them even Jack and Debbie who had become drinking buddies so they each had someone to share their pain with. Everything was good and there was more laughter from them instead of the moans of despair because they felt like they were alone and nobody out there shared their same fate.

Paula and Richard were getting along and their arguing was more playful banter than anything else. Mike had found someone that he could get along with and was happy. She might have had one terrible characteristic, but she liked Mike and he felt better when he was with her than he had with anyone else. For Mike and Nicole that's all that really mattered.

Jen and Jarrod had been seeing each other for a couple of months and when you were around them, you would have thought that they had been together for years or even married. They had found in each other what they were always looking for, the perfect complement to one another. After all the years that these people had been coming to the bar with their gripes and their unresolved issues of love it was nice to see them finally happy, but it was only a matter time.

It was only a matter of time when all hell would break loose, when all the things that they thought were good would come crashing down. I wish that I could have told them what it was really like, I wish I could've shared with them from all my years of experience what I knew to be true. I wish I could say that they did not have to go through the trenches to find what it really means to love someone, but the truth is the only way to know is to experience it firsthand. The only thing worth knowing is what we can learn from our own experience and the only way to know anything when it comes to love is to experience it all no matter how painful. I wish I could tell them that as a friend, but sometimes we have to be the silent friend who's there to comfort those that need it when they come and ask for it.

    After a few months of everybody getting back into a happy routine things started to fall apart. Even when Jack started dating again long after his divorce had been finalized disaster was about to set in. It wasn't anything he could have foreseen or anything he would have been aware of until it happened. With Jack, though, he would finally be forced to admit aloud what he had always known to be true. And so my friends would finally come to know the difference between truth, the choices we make, and the misguided notions wrapped in poor assumptions that we live by because the act tends to be safer and less painful.

∞∞∞∞∞

The first to experience what I like to call the bad voodoo was Jen and Jarrod. They had been seeing each other for only a few months, but they were getting close. They were even starting to talk about the future and what it would be like if they were married. After all, the conversation is bound to come up when you start living together– they had been spending so much time together that they started spending the night together at her place at least five or six nights a week.

One afternoon when Jarrod was off with his friends playing basketball and he had left his phone at her place he got a strange phone call from another woman. Jen answered the phone when she heard it ringing-she was partly curious who it might be and concerned that Jarrod was calling his phone to try and find it. The curiosity won out more than the concern. She answered the phone only to hear another women's voice on the other end. The voice simply identified herself as Mary and told Jen to tell Jarrod to give her a call, it was important.

Jen was a little angry-she knew it couldn't have been the police station or the woman would have said so. Jen tried not to be jealous or get suspicious, but it really didn't work; her assumptions got the better of her. She thought about it and tried to forget, but that didn't work either; all she did was get angrier. She was so angry and letting her stubborn pride take over, which affected her rationale, that when Jarrod came home he walked into the other end of an interrogation.

As he walked through the door she asked him. "You got a call from someone named Mary, is someone that I should know or did you forget to mention her?"

Jarrod didn't know how to respond. He got angry and wanted to lash out at the assertiveness in her questioning, but he also knew that it would make it worse. There was nothing he could say that wouldn't make this look bad except lie to her and that would just be worse. He calmly replied. "I know somebody named Mary and no, I've never mentioned her before."

Jen said to him. "If you're playing around with somebody else then I don't want to know about it, but if so you have a lot of nerve."

"It's not what you think."
"I don't know what to think."
"At least let me explain."

Jen gave him the opportunity to explain who Mary was, but in her stubbornness she had already decided that she probably wasn't going to believe anything he said.

About two years before they met Jarrod had been living with someone, her name was Mary and she had a three-year-old son. Jarrod had dated and lived with her for over a year, not necessarily for her, but because she had a kid who needed someone stable in his life. It was accidental in how he met Mary –she had been the witness in a drug bust. What Jarrod didn't know at the time was that she was a drug addict and it was a coincidence that she happened to be a witness in a drug bust where he was the arresting officer. She was actually going to see the dealer and it just so happened that the bust was made before she could be a part of it.

Not too far in the relationship he found out that she was a drug addict with a kid at the house who was in need of a father figure. Jarrod did the only good thing he could think of- he moved in with her and tried to get her help while taking care of her kid. She did go to rehab for a few months, but it wasn't too long after being back that she had a relapse. Jarrod would stay with her for another seven months, taking care of her son just to give him something stable. But the end finally came on the situation be. She left him because he kept trying to help her, but she didn't want it. Mary shacked up with some other guy who didn't care and within a few weeks married him.

It didn't last and Jarrod was always a last resort for her when she really needed help. The thing is Jarrod being the decent man he was couldn't turn her down especially when it came to helping her son. He was always at the top of the list when it came to emergency contacts at the pre-school because he was a police officer. He was called often even if it was just to pick him because somebody forgot. He stepped in when she needed it and when she had nowhere else to turn. She called this time because she had finally been arrested for buying drugs and child services was going to take her kid away.

Jarrod tried to explain everything about her and what the situation was with. He even pointed out that with all of Mary's mistakes and irresponsibility she did lover her son and did everything she could do to take care of him. However, it wasn't good enough and it would never be until she got over her drug addiction.

Jen looked at him after he finished and said. "It's an interesting tale, but are you sure you don't keep talking with her because there might be a chance you two could get back together."

Jarrod gave her a dirty look and replied to her. "It has nothing to do with that."

"Why didn't' you tell me about her?"

"Because I didn't think you would understand. I thought if I tried to tell you might think I was lying about having another girl on the side."

"If it's the truth then you have nothing to hide. I may not understand, but I wouldn't be mad at you for lying to me."

"It's not always that simple and to be honest- I never thought I would here from her again. If I didn't hear from her then there would be no reason to tell you."

Jen gave him an angry look and replied. "Then that shows me you're hiding something and now I wonder what else you're hiding."

Jarrod gave her an apologetic look and said. "Okay that came out wrong, what I meant to say is that I don't know if where close enough yet to know things like that about each other and so there would be no reason to tell you about her yet."

"So I'm okay to fuck and you can practically move into my house, but I don't deserve to know why some other girl might be calling you."

Jarrod didn't know what to say after that and really there was nothing he could that would make it right-he hadn't told Jen about Mary yet and it was sign of distrust. He asked Jen. "Have you told me everything yet?"

She replied. "I've told you the important things about my relationships because I trust you." She walked out of the room and gathered her things. She told Jarrod that she need some time alone or with a friend so she was leaving for while. She left and Jarrod gathered his things and went back to his place, it was obvious to him that he and Jen would not speak to each other for a few days.

Jen ended up going out for drinks with her friend Julie-it was a girl's night so they could vent about the men in their lives. It was much like years ago when Jen finally broke up with Sam and started to live her life again. Julie and Jen had their wine, and they made their complaints. They finally got it all in the open, all the lingering questions they had about why a good relationship never seemed to exist for them.

Jen asked her friend. "Do you think it's a lie if they've never told you anything about someone in their past even when you never asked about it before?"

"We're talking about men, right?"

"Yes, I haven't turned into a lesbian yet."

"I would say yes for two reasons, one they're men so they're prone to lie and the second, why would they if they didn't want to hide something deceitful or they felt like they couldn't trust you."

"The second reason is a good point, but don't we all do that."

"Sure, but women have a great excuse-we're supposed to be mysterious and make them chase us."

Jen started laughing at her friends comments. She was right in a way, but despite all the sarcasm Jen still felt guilty for being mad because she knew Jarrod was a good man and perhaps he was telling the truth. Jen was sure that Jarrod had his reasons and maybe one of those was realizing that as stubborn as she was he felt like she wouldn't completely understand.

Julie asked her friend. "How much do you really care about Jarrod?"

"I like him a lot in fact I lov…"

"Oh my god, "Julie said cutting Jen off, "You're going to say it aren't you?"

"Yes I am."

"You haven't known this guy that long, are you crazy?"

"You introduced us because you thought he would be perfect for me, aren't you happy that I'm in love with him-isn't this what you wanted."

"Of course I do, but I also thought the Pizza guy was perfect for you too. I just don't think you can say I love you to a guy when you've only known him for three months."

Jen laughed at her friend's sarcastic comments; Julie had a point, but what does time have to do when it comes to love. Jen said. "I don't think time has anything to do with it-I know what I have and I know what I had."

"Then you don't need any answers from me, you seem to already know what you're going to do and more power to you because not everybody can figure it out."

"You don't have it all figured out?"

"Hell no, after a week I'm usually bored with a guy and that's when I kick him out of my life. It's the long term that I can't figure out-that's why I'm usually on the prowl and why I usually give terrible advice."

Jen laughed again at her friend's sarcasm and then said. "Your advice is not that terrible, at least it's funny."

"The only thing I can tell you Jen is if you truly love Jarrod then go home and fix this with him - it's not worth losing something special. Besides you haven't been totally honest with him-you haven't told him about Brian."

Jen sighed because Julie was right; even she was afraid to tell something delicate from her past not believing he would understand. Julie and Jen finished their drinks while having a few more laughs before they went home. They both knew the answers to the things most important in their lives, but they had to confirm them aloud with one another as friends often do. It was always better to hear a friend say it out loud so you know that you're not alone.

The next day after Jen was done with work she went home –she was going to call Jarrod so she could straighten everything out. She had to be honest and she knew that she had to have faith that there would be understanding. She arrived home to find Jarrod at her place packing up his things. She was surprised to see him and after seeing the angry look in his eyes she knew that something was terribly wrong.

Jarrod just looked at her with contempt; this time he was the one hurt by the secrets that she kept. She asked him "what's wrong, why are packing your things. I wasn't going to kick you out; I just needed a day to get over being angry."

Jarrod looked at her with his penetrating eyes that bore hatred deep inside of her. He said. "I know, but I'm not packing my things because of that."

"Then why are you?"

"I'm leaving because of your secret."

"What are you talking about?" She asked him even though she already knew the answer.

"When I got here this afternoon to surprise you with flowers, you had a visitor. Brian was here and we ended up having a nice chat."

Jen tried to lighten the mood by adding humor to it. She replied. "You didn't do the whole cop thing and rough him up did you?"

"No, but was pretty truthful. Apparently, he came by to see if he could talk you into coming back and being his sex partner. He said he missed you in the bedroom."

Jen had a horrified look on her face. Her secret had caught up with her. It wasn't that having a sexual relationship with someone was that bad – it was the fact that she didn't tell him because a part of her was ashamed. She was afraid of what he might think. Jarrod and Jen they were both victims of their own poor assumptions and lack of faith.

Jarrod Replied. "I don't care who you've slept with, but how dare you get mad at me and make me feel guilty for not telling you something when you can't be honest with me. We both have our own secrets. I guess it's true what good are we as a couple when we can't be honest with one another."

"I'm sorry."

"I know, but it's not good enough. He's not even a decent guy, did you know that he had a felony assault charge out against him"

"What did you do, run a background check on him after you met him?"

"Of course I did, I'm a cop. I wanted to see how much trouble you might have been in?"

"I see you're real trusting."

"And you're one to talk."

Jen just gave him a dirty look and then he walked past her with his boxes in hand. He didn't say anything to her as he walked out and he didn't even turn around to look at her. Jen just watched as he walked down the stairs until he was out of site and that was it they didn't speak to each other again. She tried to be mad after he left, but all she could was cry and Jarrod, well, he too was sad. He was even mad although though he tried to cover it up in anger.

∞∞∞∞∞

Jack ordered a cup of coffee from the waitress at the diner where he was waiting for his brother Richard. It was their usually meeting for breakfast at their favorite diner. They would catch up and discuss the current events within their lives. Richard was late as usual, but after about fifteen minutes and two cups of coffee, Richard finally showed up. He walked through the door in a hurry and sat down with an excitement that portrayed that everything was right in the world. Jack looked at him and said.

"You're energetic this morning; did you get some really good sex last night?"

"As a matter of fact, I did and it was pretty special."

"What did she do - some new trick that you've never done before?"

"No, it was pretty simple. But it was great waking up next to her."

"So who is this girl or do you not remember her name."

Richard laughed and replied to his brother. "You're funny, but I didn't forget her name and I don't think I ever could."

"That's good to hear." Jack said in kind of a disdained tone. "I'm glad you had a wonderful night."

"You know maybe you should think about getting out there again, it's been a long while since the divorce was finalized."

"Maybe, but I don't know if I'm quite ready."

Richard gave Jack a dirty look and said. "You can at least get laid-at this point you need it."

"Is that all you think about-there's more to life than sex."

"Maybe, but not in your case. I'm just saying you can at least fulfill that primal need- I know you have it."

Jack took a sip of coffee and gave his brother a dirty look right back. After the ordering of breakfast and a brief rundown on how the Cubs were doing Jack asked a serious question to Richard. "So I heard an interesting rumor that you and Paula were seeing each other, is that true"

"You mean you heard an interesting rumor from Debbie?"

"Maybe!"

"Come on man, I already know that she's your drinking buddy these days, which I think is cool."

"So what of it? Answer the question little brother.'

"Yes, I am seeing her and it's a good thing."

Jack just smiled at his brother and then started quietly laughing. His brother fell victim to it- the part of life where we start caring for someone more than ourselves. He was falling in love and didn't even realize it. Jack finally asked. "Is that who you were with last night"

"Maybe, but it's not that big of a deal."

"Yes it is, but you used to hate her and she used to hate you; now you two are rarely apart."

"How do you know that…oh, right, Debbie, your drinking buddy?"

"It doesn't matter how I know, what matters is that you're falling for her and you're life is changing in a big way."

"Thank you Trinidad." Richard replied sarcastically. "I like Paula and I do see her a lot, but that doesn't mean my life is changing in some dramatic way."

Jack looked at his brother with a serious look and asked him "Are you sleeping around with anyone else?"

Richard said. "No, but that doesn't mean I won't sleep with someone else. Paula and I are not serious?"

"Maybe, but you don't want to be with anyone else, which means you're falling for Paula. I know this because it's the same way I felt about Sara when we first met and I eventually married her if you recall."

Richard scoffed a bit at the notion, but there was a certain truth to it and he knew it for anything was possible. Richard just changed the subject and over breakfast they caught up and talked about other things. Finally Richard got up to leave, shook his brother's hand and said to him. "Seriously man you need to go out on a date, you really need to get laid, its time. Ask Debbie to set you up with someone –she knows lots of desperate, kinky girls that will give you a night to remember."

Jack laughed at his brother as he walked out of the diner. He knew he was right and even though he wasn't wildly excited about it he asked Debbie the next day to set him up with someone-even a night of just sex might be good. The next day he saw Debbie at The Matador and sure enough he had a girl for him to meet. Debbie had met her by accident at work thinking she was gay and would be good for her, but to her depressing surprise, she wasn't.

Debbie joked with Jack that this girl was probably too kinky for her, but would be good enough for him because it was a crazy person in bed that he really needed. She was right to a point. The next day met this girl for dinner, whose name just happened to be Sara, but with an H. She seemed nice and she was the perfect girl in bed that night for Jack, she was just what he needed after being out of the game for so long. After she spent the night with Jack they agreed to see each other again. Jack and Sarah with an H spent all day Sunday together, part of it was in bed and part of it was out on the town for they both loved Chicago on a Sunday afternoon. For Jack it was great because even though it was something new and something he had not felt in a long time, it was something he needed. He thought to himself, she could be the one he needed to forget his ex-wife even if some of Sara with an H's stories were starting to conflict with one another.

After Sunday, they parted and she gave him her number, another thing that had been a long time for Jack. They agreed to meet for dinner the next day at a favorite Italian joint they both loved. He showed up first and waited, but she never showed. He waited for an hour and she still never showed. Jack was worried, but more importantly he was worried that his luck had run out-it had. Jack called the number and to his surprise, a male voice answered the phone.

The male voice was Sara with an H's husband. He asked Jack who he was and Jack explained that she was her date and he had met her over the weekend, when she didn't show for their dinner date he got worried and called the number she left him. The male voice just simply replied, "Oh, not again!"

His wife was schizophrenic and would periodically go off her medication. She would also be gone for days at a time, meeting strangers and most of them just happened to be men. The male voice also explained that as much as he wanted to help his wife, he loved her too much to put her in hospital. Apparently, she had done this before and she even had a child years before, which he didn't know for sure whether it was his or not. Jack could admire his devotion, but also thought he was crazier than she was for not stopping that nonsense. Jack hung up the phone and felted embarrassed for what he had endured. He had finally hit a new low-he had slept with a "schizophrenic" who was married with a child. It didn't matter if she couldn't remember that one important fact or if he didn't know it at the time-he had hit a low point to where all he could do was feel repulsed by his actions.

  The next day he saw Debbie at The Matador and told her and Trinidad what happened. She couldn't help but laugh. It's funny how many people can actually say that they dated or slept with a schizophrenic without knowing it and the situation never involved a police report or a restraining order. It took a while for the laughter to stop among Debbie and Trinidad, even Mina Trinidad's wife laughed a little bit when she heard the story. When the laughter had finally stopped, Debbie told Jack that she would make it up to him by finding someone else that wasn't insane or at least not quite as insane.

Jack was beginning to figure out that, the dating scene had changed since the last time he was out there and that it wasn't going to be as easy as he thought. Although, Debbie did remind him that it could be worse; he could have gone through the same situation that Mike did - his date trying to kill him. That's when you know you've hit rock bottom especially when you didn't do anything to deserve the attempt on your life except for just being in the wrong place at the wrong time.

Debbie did have someone else in mind for Jack; it was a girl that she worked with and she was very sweet while having a very sarcastic sense of humor. For Debbie it was too bad that she wasn't a lesbian or Debbie would have been after her like fat person on a pizza after a weight watchers event. The woman's name was Rebecca and while at the bar having a drink with Jack she called her friend and set the date up for the weekend. Rebecca was another love torn soul who had endured her fair share of rotten men in her life and bad breakups, but she was always faithful that second chances would come her way so she welcomed any chance to make her faith a reality.

Jack was not that excited about going on another date, he was a little reluctant to say yes and even had to get advice from his favorite bartender before agreeing to it. Jack spoke up and asked. "Trinidad, what do you think, you think I should take another chance?"

"You should try anything that gets you to stop pining away in my bar and waiting for a cure to the depressing love that you only find in romance novels if you know what I mean."

"Yeah, but depressing people like me put money in your pocket. You'd miss someone like me"

"Sure. Although what I really want is your money, but getting it from you is a lot more fun when you're in a good mood?"

Debbie laughed and then replied. "He's right, take a chance on another date, you might actually find happiness and getting laid wouldn't hurt either."

Jack looked at her and replied with sarcasm, "This from the girl who is still waiting for Paula to come back and be gay with her?"

"I still date other people. I still take my chances and there is no argument that you can make which won't make you sound like a pussy."

Jack smirked a bit at Debbie because she was right and so he agreed to go out with another one of her friends. It was a few days later when he met Rebecca for dinner. She was nice and they had a good time, none of the usual first date bullshit where they tried to impress each other and make themselves out to be something that they weren't. Jack and Rebecca just talked as if they were the best of friends. They knew a little bit about each other from what Debbie has said about each of them to the other.

Overall it was nice for the both of them; Jack didn't lie about what he was looking for when it came to finding someone new and Rebecca was as direct as one could be. She pulled no punches about what she was looking for. She wanted to share her life with someone and she was on a quest to find the perfect guy for herself. Jack and Rebecca did click, and maybe in another life they would have been perfect for each other, but we're all victims of circumstance even when we don't realize it you.

After dinner, they went back to his place. The date had gone well so she felt comfortable enough going back with Jack to his place when he invited her. She was attracted to him and in the back of her mind she thought that it could be the perfect night for them to sleep with one another even though it was the first date. Jack just liked the company-he hadn't gotten used to Sara not being there.

Jack opened a bottle of wine so he and Rebecca could enjoy the rest of the night. Jack was hesitant to make a move on her and finally after about twenty minutes and a couple of glasses of wine Rebecca took it upon herself to start something. She put her glass down and leaned in closer hoping that he would get the hint and kiss her. Jack didn't, but it didn't stop her-she leaned in and kissed him. Even though Jack wasn't the one who started it, he went along with it and started kissing her. That went on for a few minutes and she wondered if he would start to take her clothes off or lead her into the bedroom, but he didn't.

Again, she had to start it and so she did –she started to unbutton his shirt. For whatever reason Jack couldn't go along with it, he stopped her and apologized. Rebecca wasn't mad; she just smiled and asked him. "How long has it been since your divorce was final?"

"If I tell you then you'll really be mad at me or laugh at me."

"No I won't. You have nothing to be ashamed of, what has it been, 6 months a year?"

"It's been a year."

"Sometimes it takes awhile to get back into the swing of things, but here's the real question-do you still love her and don't lie, at this point it wouldn't do you any good."

Jack thought about it for a moment and then replied. "I don't know if I still love her, but I still love the idea of her?"

Rebecca laughed and she said. "We always like the idea of someone, because we don't like to be alone, but it's a cheap excuse for not being brave enough to admit our true feelings."

Jack scoffed a bit at her comment and said. "Maybe you're right and I don't know if I've ever really thought about it that way."

Rebecca smiled again at Jack and said. "Well I'm not trying to put you on the spot, but whether you admit it or not you're still in love with her-you have to be, because I don't think you're gay and I'm practically throwing myself at you, which you're not responding to…it's okay to admit that you still have feelings for your ex-wife."

Jacked smiled and laughed to himself, He said to Rebecca. "I think there is a part of me that will always love her."

"It's not the real answer, but close enough. I think when you have a history together and when the separation is not always clear cut then you can't help but feel something for the other person even if it's the doubt processing your thoughts."

Jack smiled at Rebecca and she gave him a hug. She wanted him to know that she understood. She felt empathy for him for she too, had lost a loved one that she never quite got over. She said all she could do was learn to forget. Jack on the other hand couldn't forget and without saying it aloud he did admit it with a smile He admitted that he was still in love with Sara and he knew that all could do was live with his regret for what had happened. For the rest of the evening Jack and Rebecca just talked, they talked about past loves and found a comfort in the sympathy of a stranger

∞∞∞∞∞∞

That same night while Jack was out on his date with Rebecca Debbie was having a different sort of night. It started just like every other night at The Matador. She got her drink and mingled with other people, flirting and giving the sign that she was looking for someone. Debbie liked to tease and sometimes it was too strong. She liked to let the young women know that she was smarter and had more control over the young in the bar even though she was thirty-something now. It was her fun little game and she never stayed with anyone long enough to give them the impression that they had a chance with her. Her real desire was the younger females because it was all about bringing them out of their denial.

The way Debbie saw it, all young women were in denial about being with another woman-they all wanted to because sometimes a woman knows how to push the proper buttons better than a man. Even if it was not going to be a lifestyle, women still needed to be with other women just to find that sensuality that was lacking with their male counter parts. So it was always a quest of Debbie's to bring women out of their denial and to tease the young men she met into submission so by the end of the night they wanted her so bad that they would give her anything she wanted.

With all the people she was talking to that night at the bar she spent most of the evening with a group of young college students-three women and four men who were not necessarily together as couples. Two of the men seemed really interested in Debbie and she flirted with them quite a bit even though she was paying close attention to a young petite blond sitting in the group.

Debbie could just sense that the young blond needed to be with a woman and experience something different. One of the guys that seemed interested in Debbie was scary in a way and she felt a little uncomfortable around him. He just had a look that put an uneasy feeling in you and he looked a little unstable like he could snap at any moment. Maybe it was the few drinks he had that made him seem that way, but still there was something about him.

Debbie had fun with the group and when the night was over mainly because the young blonde couldn't come out of her shell yet Debbie excused her and said goodbye. After being outside for a few minutes while trying to find her car keys the man who made her feel uneasy came up to her and asked if she needed him to driver her home. She said no and quickly tried to get in her car that was parked around the corner in an alleyway where nobody from the bar could see. The man insisted and not in a comforting sort of way that said I care about your safety. This time when she said no she yelled a little bit hoping that he would get the hint.

The man didn't get the point. He called her a bitch and cursed her for being a tease and then acted like he was going to walk off. When he started to walk off Debbie turned around, taking her eyes off him and that's when it happened. It happened so quick that she didn't see it coming. The man pushed her hard against the car, it caused Debbie to be knocked unconscious. That was all she could remember happening before waking up in her car in a deserted parking lot 10 miles from The Matador.

Debbie was bruised and felt a sharp pain in her face and chest and that's when she noticed her pants halfway down her legs. The she felt the pain in her vagina and the realization finally set in. Debbie had been assaulted and raped. When the realization of what happened finally hit she froze. She felt the pain, the disgust, and the utter humiliation of what happened. That's when she became limp and catatonic from the shock of everything. She couldn't even scream for help, she just sat there in her car in pain, and in tears.

An ambulance would arrive thirty minutes later and that only happened because of a good-hearted soul who happened to be walking by and saw her. He was the one who called 911 emergency. Debbie hardly moved even when the paramedics worked on her-she was still frozen with shock. There was a hospital near-by so it didn't take long for her and the ambulance to arrive. She was immediately worked on by a doctor as they got her a bed in the ER. After the rape kit was done they didn't find any significant damage, just bruising and it was mostly on her face. The rapist didn't force her repeatedly from what the doctor could find, but it would talk a long time to heal. There was a female nurse working that night who stayed by Debbie's side like a caring mother for her sick child. She felt a real warm spot for Debbie and empathized over what she had been through. The nurse knew that with a patient like Debbie it would take that extra sense of compassion that only a good nurse can.

Debbie didn't say a word all through the examinations she just nodded when asked a question; it was all she could do as she was still in shock. About an hour, after she arrived at the hospital Paula arrived, she was Debbie's emergency contact since her family lived in another state and the hospital found Paula's information in her purse which luckily was at the scene-the creep who committed that horrific act had left the purse there. Paula was in tears when she saw Debbie in her room all bruised and beaten.

Resting her hand on Debbie's head and grabbing her hand to comfort her she said to her friend. "Debbie honey, I'm here and I'm not going anywhere."

Debbie didn't respond, all she did was blink and nod slightly at Paula, but there were tears in her eyes as her memory of what happened came back. Paula responded. "Honey, it's okay, you're going to be okay."

Debbie finally spoke for the first time as the nurse who was taking care of her was standing there checking her IV. She said. "It's not going to be okay, it never will be."

"You don't mean that" Paula replied.

"I was a fool, this is all my fault."

"Don't say that, this is not your fault. There's no need to blame yourself."

"It is my fault, I caused this crime because I was a tease."

"Do you know who did this to you Debbie?"

"Of course I do, he was at the bar tonight and I was teasing him."

"Then you tell the police and they will get him. They'll put him jail, I can make sure they do that."

"No you can't. You can't do anything even though you could have prevented this."

Paula paused in shock at what Debbie was saying. Even the nurse raised an eyebrow to the comment. Paula just thought Debbie was still in shock, but it wasn't the case. She was angry and hurt and in that moment of tragedy the truth was spilling over beyond her playful sarcasm.

Paula had to ask Debbie what she meant. She simply asked to get at the truth like the lawyer inside of her. "What could I have done?"

"If you were with me I wouldn't have been in a situation where this would happen?"

"Debbie I had plans tonight and you knew that –I can't be with you every night."

"I know you were with Richard tonight, but if you and I were together as a couple then this would not have happened."

Paula shed a few tears at the shocking and hurtful things that Debbie was saying. She hurt for her friend and for the fact that she could not be with her friend even though Debbie was in love with her. She hurt because the shock and anger over this tragedy was turning into blame towards her. Paula responded to her. "I'm sorry, but I've been honest with you, I love you as my friend. I don't love you that way. I can't be a lesbian. I don't know what else I can do, but be honest with you."

Debbie gave Paula a dirty look and replied. "You say you can be honest with me, but have you been honest with Richard about who you're really in love with and the affair you had with him even though he's married. How do I know that you're honesty with me is not just to hurt me."

Paula couldn't say anything to her friend, she knew even though Debbie was in pain that she was right. Paula didn't know how to respond to her friends comment. All she told Debbie was that she would wait outside and check on her later. Debbie just screamed at her in anger and told her to get out and not to come back. The nurse escorted Paula out of the room and Paula walked down the hospital hallway towards the doorway with the sounds of Debbie's screams ringing in her ears.

∞∞∞∞∞

    Paula had not spoken to Debbie in a few days, not since the hospital. Debbie's mother did call her and let her know that she had been released from the hospital and was now safe at home getting well. About every few years, they went through a huge fight and would spend about a month not speaking to each to each other, but unlike most fights Paula wasn't so sure that they would get past it and be friends again.
    Everyone was concerned about Debbie and Jack even checked up on her every day so most of what Paula knew about Debbie's recovery came from Jack. She was concerned about her friend and

those thoughts weighed on her every day, but it was mostly what she had said about not telling the truth. Paula knew that her and Richard had their dirty little secrets, but as close as they might be getting Paula thought that they weren't there yet. It wasn't truth time yet because they still didn't know where this was going. All she knew was that she could just be one of Richard's little flings. Everybody needed someone to relieve their sexual tension so it wouldn't have been that big of a deal if that's what was really going on.

    Richard and Paula just went about their usually routine, which at this point was spending most of their time together. They were even seeing each other out in public a lot more; their sordid love affair wasn't really a secret anymore. So with this new found meaning in their relationship they actually started dating, doing what real couples do. Paula had an office black tie party to go to and her date would be Richard. It wasn't something that Richard would usually go to, but he did it anyway just to be with her. He still couldn't admit it, but he pretty much wanted to spend every moment he could with her.

    They went to the party and it was nice, but it was boring. Richard made the comment that at least they had free booze, which is always a plus at a party. The food was nice and the speeches made by the partners of the firm were, well, pompous and dull. About an hour into the party when everybody was good and drunk, Paula's boss pulled her aside into a private room, he was the one that she was in love with and had been having an affair with. He was drunk, but he wanted to talk to her and she didn't have the strength to say no. Richard was mingling with people from the office that knew him as a reporter in Chicago so he didn't notice Paula gone.

Her boss looked at her and said. "Paula, honey I miss you. Why can't we see each other again?"

"I told you," she replied. "I'm not going to continue this with you while you're still married. We've talked about this before."

"Look I am going to file for divorce. I'm ready to leave her now and I want to be with you."

"Okay, but how I do I know that you're not just saying that."

"Well let me prove it to you." He leaned in, kissed her and she didn't stop him. She couldn't because deep down she still loved him and would still be with him if she could. Richard was trying find her and he did at the exact moment she kissed him back. She didn't do it for very long, but that's not what Richard saw.

He didn't get mad and start a fight with the guy although he wanted to. Paula saw him and immediately stopped what she was doing. She walked away with Richard and just told him her boss was drunk. Richard knew that wasn't the whole truth, but he didn't say anything until they left and went home. They left the party soon after that incident.

When they got home, Richard finally asked. "So what was that all about with your boss?"

"It was nothing, he was drunk and he tried to get romantic with me."

"There's more to it than that isn't there?"

"Okay, you're reading too much into this."

"Yeah, I tend to do that when I'm sniffing out the truth and I'm not entirely convinced yet."

Paula gave him a dirty look and said. "I wouldn't lie to you."

Richard looked at her with a seriousness that he didn't have very often, only when he knew people were lying to him. It was a journalistic thing and with all the years he had been on the job as a reporter he could always tell when people weren't telling the truth. He said to her. "You're not telling me something."

"Richard its nothing, don't play the jealous role."

"I'm not jealous. I just want to know why you keep skirting the issue, There something about that guy. Do you have a history together?"

She gave him a look that tried to shake off the question; she was trying to avoid an answer because she still don't want to tell him the truth. Finally, she said. "Quit being paranoid, there is nothing between me and that guy."

"Sure there is or you wouldn't try to change the subject so quickly. Why can't you just tell me?"

Paula tried to give him another bullshit answer in the hopes of changing the subject. Before she could finish her sentence Richard got mad and slammed a kitchen chair on the floor. She was startled and gave him a horrified look.

Richard replied. "Quit giving me bullshit, what's the deal with you and that guy.

"All right fine then, you want to know the truth?"

"It would be nice."

"I had an affair with him for over a year. I finally ended it last year."

Richard was dumbfounded, he never imagined that Paula would actually have an affair with a married man. He didn't know what to say, but he finally got something out. He asked her. "Why did it end?"

"He wouldn't leave his wife."

"Did you really think he would while having an affair with you?"

"Yes, I did."

"I can't believe you're that fucking stupid."

Paula finally got angry and it showed on her face. She replied. "You're out of line, we all make mistakes and men do leave their wives for other women all the time."

"Not if they have the best of both worlds. He's a man, if get away with something he will and sleeping with two women is good example of that. You can't see that."

"How was I supposed to know that he would never keep his promises with me?"

"You know what's even worse? It never occurred to you that if he was willing to cheat on his wife for you then he would be willing to cheat on you for someone else."

Paula didn't say anything, there was nothing to say, she had screwed up in Richard's eyes and there was nothing else she could to change that. Richard said to her. "I don't mind people making mistakes because you're right we all fuck up. What I want to know is, how could you be so dumb as to think that this was a good idea?"

She said in a whispery tone. "I made a mistake, nothing more."

"Why did you try and lie to me?"

"Because it wasn't any of your business. You don't tell me everything."

"How do you know I don't?"

"Have you told me all about your flings even the one's you still have from time to time when you don't get to see me."

"I'm not going to tell you about my sexual conquests, but if you ask then I will. As for the flings I still have, I haven't been with anyone else since you and I started actually dating. I wasn't going to cheat on you."

Paula paused for a moment while she was starting to realize that Richard had actually been more honest with her than she with him. He had also been more truthful with her when it came to them forging a relationship together.

Richard asked her "Are you still having an affair with him."

"No."

"Are you in love with him?"

"Does it matter?"

"If it was just for sex then I would understand, but love is a whole different can of worms?"

"Then you won't like the answer."

Richard gave her an angry look and said. "If you could, would you get back with him, I mean if he had left his wife."

Paula didn't want to say anything because she knew what the answer would do to Richard. She knew that he had feelings for her, more that he had for any other woman. Richard asked her the same question again. She said yes and all Richard could do in his anger was push over the kitchen table and walk out slamming the door behind him.

∞∞∞∞∞∞

For the next few nights Richard stayed in and didn't go out, he was too drunk to go anywhere. Mike tried to talk to him, but he knew the best thing to do was to leave Richard alone and let him sort it out for himself. Finally, after a few days Richard went out, he went to a bachelor party for a friend at the newspaper. As he was getting ready Mike asked him. "Are you ever going to call her or are you just going to keep being mad?"

Richard gave him a dirty look and said. "That's a question I should answer when I'm at least sober. For now, I'm going out to get laid. A bachelor party sounds like the best thing for me."

"Okay if you say so, but I think you should at least call Paula and try to get everything out in the open."

"She'll probably just lie again. So how about you, you seeing Nicole tonight?"

"No, unfortunately she has to work."

Richard got up after putting his shoes on to comb his hair and put some cologne on. He looked at Mike and said. "You know, I think it's about time I meet her. You've been seeing her for a few months now, its time she met you friends, don't you think?"

"It would be a little too much reality for her, under the circumstances it's going to take some time before we get to the whole meeting the friend's thing."

"Fine, suit yourself, but it's going to be something real then she has to meet you friends. I can see why she wouldn't have met your family yet, but your friends are a different story."

Mike laughed at him and said. "We'll get there."

"Remember," Richard replied as he put his wallet in his back pocket, "your friends are the best thing you have going for you, they're the ones that will look out for you. It's another reason I think we should meet her."

Mike said. "Don't rush it, it will happen. You'll meet her before you know it." Richard patted his friend on the shoulder and left for the evening.

The party was somewhat fun and the talent that was there made it a bachelor party that no one was going to forget. There were strippers and hookers that still had their looks which made for one interesting night. Richard mostly drank beer during the night and wasn't getting into all the pussy that was there. Some of it was quite literally for some of the patrons. His friend James spared no expense to have a good time before his wedding. The party had topless waitresses with plenty of tits and glamour, and while it was mixed with booze, some of the men would get a little grabby.

There was one particular waitress that Richard took notice of a stunning redhead with piercing green eyes. Richard had always liked redheads and when someone drunker than him was bothering her, he intervened. He pushed the guy out of the way and let her get on with the evening. Richard couldn't keep his eyes off her all night an about an hour later when things were quieting down she came up to Richard to thank him. She said she hadn't forgotten him and wanted to thank him for what he did.

Richard introduced himself as they started chatting and she introduced herself as Nicole. Yeah, it was that Nicole. She sometimes freelanced as a topless waitress for bachelor parties; it was a job where she could make good money without having to sleep with someone. He didn't know who she was and she didn't know who he was so it was only natural to chat each other up. It was a little weird under the circumstances, but sometimes things like that do happen.

Richard and Nicole started talking and they go to the usual conversation of dating. The asked each other about their relationships and if there was somebody at home waiting for them. Nicole didn't tell him the truth, it was one of those rules - you never bring your personal life into it. For people like her they're always somebody else.

Maybe it was because he was drunk, but Richard told her what had happened with him and Paula trying to seek comfort in the arms of a stranger. She had started drinking by that point as the party came to a close. Most of the guests had passed out and the rest of the talent had gone home. She stayed behind to talk with Richard, the way she saw it, he was the most lonely man in the room and in need of a friend. Not the kind you get for a night, but a stranger in the shadow of a friend that could sympathize.

Somewhere in the conversation it happened, about the time he noticed her tattoo, a Celtic cross that fit right in the small of her back above the "panty" line. He noticed the tattoo and leaned in to kiss her as she was telling him why she had it. It was a normal situation and she would have stopped him, but for some reason she didn't. She wanted to sympathize with him because she had been where he was and he was too damn drunk to know what he was doing so in her mind the only thing she could do was make him feel better and for now kissing him was it.

Since he was too drunk to go anywhere she got him into one of the hotel rooms that were vacant where the party was being held. She found a spare bed and helped him to it so she could put him to sleep, but he kept kissing her and feeling the softness of her skin. Against her better judgment, she didn't stop him. She was in a trance because he was a nice guy; a lonely and confused guy, but still a nice guy. And so it happened, she slept with him and there were no excuses for why she did it; something in her wanted to And for all the logic that we can come up with there are times that nothing makes sense and seems right.

They woke up next morning to sound of knocking by the chambermaid. Both of them were surprised, but didn't say anything. There was nothing to say. They got up and said goodbye ignoring what had happened and trying to forget the regret that would happen later. Richard thought about introducing himself since he could not remember whether he had the night before, but under the circumstances, it wouldn't be the best thing to do. He just said goodbye as she walked out the door and thanked her for listening. He didn't even realize and nor did she the ramifications of what they did.

Richard arrived home about an hour later just as Mike was preparing some breakfast. Mike could tell his friend was hung over and so without anything being said he made Richard a cup of coffee and some eggs. Mike asked how the party was and Richard just nodded his head with a sarcastic smile. Mike said to Richard. "So it was one of those nights."

"It was wild, but I didn't participate that much. I just got drunk as you can see."

"You didn't even get laid last night, that's got to be a first for you at one of these parties."

"I didn't say that, I still managed to get some."

Mike laughed and said. "I should have known that you weren't going to pine away for Paula. There certainly isn't any down time for you when it comes to breakups and hookups."

Richard said to his friend. "It's not like we were serious or exclusive. I can sleep with whoever I want, guilt free."

"Maybe you were getting serious with her."

Richard replied in an angry tone. "We all make mistakes."

Mike asked him who it was and Richard went on to explain about the girl he met who listened to him complain about love and then ended up screwing later. He described Nicole right down to her tattoo, which he thought was cool, and her piercing green eyes. He couldn't stop talking about how sexy she was and what perfect breasts she had. Those few details caught Mike's attention and he gave Richard a horrified look. Mike asked him if she had a name and Richard just replied that he didn't know.

Mike asked Richard to describe her in more detail from the sound of her voice and how she talked to the way she wore her hair. There were certain things about Nicole that made her stand out, she didn't talk like most people for she had her own peculiar way of communicating. It was something unique like a southern twang, but with a northern accent. And there was a certain way she wore her beautiful red hair; she sometimes wore it down, but most of the time she wore it up giving a stylish look where on most women it looked like they just got done working out.

As Richard kept describing her he began to realize why Mike was horrified, he soon realized that even though he had never seen Nicole the woman he was with last night was her. Then he realized how Mike had always described her; the details of her were the same as Mike's when it came to the things that Made Nicole beautiful. It had never occurred to Richard that this could happen because what would be the odds, but bad luck just happened to be on their side. Mike asked Richard if the woman he was with had a tattoo and Richard replied yes. Mike asked what it was and Richard said it was a Celtic cross.

Richard didn't know what to say; Mike had even more of a horrified look than his friend and then he asked Richard why. Richard couldn't say anything. Mike brushed past Richard while also pushing him out of the way in anger and walked out the door. Mike was still in a state of disbelief and he had to find out the truth from her so he went to see Nicole.

Along the way to her apartment he tried to clear his head so when he talked to her he wouldn't be so angry, but nothing he thought of could calm him down. He arrived at her door and pounded away in anger. When Nicole opened the door, she replied. "You don't have to break my door down, you know I'll let you in."

Mike looked at her in the same horrified look as he had with Richard and then asked her. "What happened last night?"

"I thought we agreed that you would never ask me about work?"

"Who did you sleep with last night?"

"It's none of your business, I don't discuss my work with you."

Mike slammed his hand on the counter top in her kitchen and asked. "Do you know who you slept with last night, I don't care about your clients, but do you even know who you slept with last night?"

Nicole gave him an angry look and replied. "How do you even know that I slept with someone last night?"

"Because my roommate and best friend said he slept with someone last night at the party he went to and he described you perfectly."

She got a horrified look because she knew there was a chance that it was true and she also knew that what she did last night would also come back to haunt her. She didn't know what to say, but she finally mustered a question. "Is your roommate named Richard and someone who just had a bad breakup."

Mike replied. "Yes." Then he asked her. "Is it true?"

Nicole knew that lying wouldn't fix it and would probably just make things worse to the point that he couldn't' trust her even though he wouldn't trust her anyway after this. She said to him "Yes it's true."

Mike broke the glass that was sitting on the counter by slamming it against the wall and cursed Nicole for her actions. She was frightened for she had never seen him this way. Then he asked Nicole, "did you charge him?"

She looked at him with solemn look and said. "Does it really matter, I still slept with him and you have no right to ask me that?"

"Sure I do, he's my friend and he should be off limits if you care about me."

"I didn't know who he was and he needed a friend even if it was just a stranger for a night."

"That's not good enough, you still slept with him and being a call girl doesn't make it all right or forgivable. I can only understand to a point."

"What does that mean, is this where you going to try to change me now, you going to make me see the error of my ways."

Mike gave her a hateful look, something that he had never done before and said. "I won't be with you if you can't change your life, not anymore."

    She replied in a sorrowful tone. "And I can't be with someone that would ask me to change my life without any compassion or understanding."

    "Then we're done and I don't want to know you." Mike started to walk out the door as Nicole responded back. "If you walk out the door then don't come back. You don't get a second chance with me."

    Mike gave her the same hateful look and replied. "I don't need one with you. I don't plan on having to use it with you." He reached for his wallet and pulled out a fifty-dollar bill. He then said to her as he put the money on the counter "here you go, I'll cover my friend's night with you, a fifty should do it."

    Nicole started to cry. And in her anger and sorrow towards Mike she said just two words "Fuck You."

    That was it Mike walked out the door and never looked back. He didn't even want to think about her. He was like all of his friends, no use for sorrow and maybe with a little bit of time, the anger could be pushed away.

So that was it with Mike, Richard, Jack, Sara, Paula, Debbie, Jen, Jarrod, and Nicole; they had all gone down a dark path where all they could do was hurt each other without remorse. It was the ugly side of love and it's only found in the trenches. It's a villain that robs you with your back turned and pushes you into the deep dark abyss with no one to hear your screams for salvation. With all of my friends, it was what they would have to go through to find any kind of happiness. They would come to a place where they would be forced to make a choice. We all come to that place eventually where the only chance we have left in order to survive is to make the hard choice.

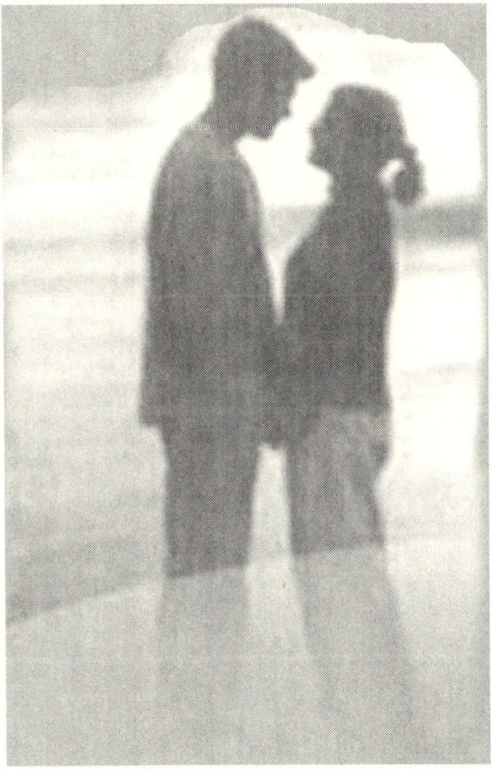

7

The Choices We Make

Anger, betrayal, and broken hearts; it's a story we all know and something that we have all lived at one time. It's not fiction, it's not a soap opera, or some trashy romance, its real life. All that we are left with are the questions of why, why us, why do we have to walk through this. Then comes the choice, the choice of whether to go on living, or whether we let what happens destroy us. It's the same old story told a thousand times and it never gets easier. If you walk into a place like *The Matador* you will see it time and time again. You people pouring out their sorrows over a drink so they don't have to remember the next day only to find that the problem never went away.

For Jack, Richard, Jen, Jarrod, Paula, Sara, Debbie, Mike and Nicole the same old story had finally happened. Now it could be said that everything worked out in the end, but that's just something you could say. The truth is life doesn't end like some fairy tale and romance doesn't happen like something you would read in a book. All of them were beginning to figure that out, but more importantly they were figuring out that what happened to them was their own doing and it was done by the choices they made.

By now, nobody was really talking to each other. Jack and Sara had not said a word to each other since the divorce and Jack still tried to ignore the fact that Sara was getting married again. Richard and Paula didn't have any contact with each other and Mike had moved out of the apartment that he and Richard shared. Debbie and Paula had not spoken to each other since she had last visited the hospital and Debbie rebuked her for being selfish in their friendship. As for Jen and Jarrod, they too, had not called or emailed each other since the day all their lies came to the surface. Nicole, well, she disappeared and Mike knew that about her because he went back to her apartment to find her, but she was gone.

The months passed and the silence among friends continued as they all went through the motions trying to ignore their hurt. To make things worse they were all too stubborn and too prideful to do anything about it, but that's usually when some of life's little accidents happen and we are forced to deal with our painful issues. So that's how it happened for these lost souls and it happened one by one until they all found themselves in dark places within their lives

The first thing that happened was an accidental meeting of chance between Jen, Debbie, and Jack. After about six months had passed Debbie was back in The Matador waiting on her drinking buddy Jack so they could drown their sorrows together as usual. Jen walked in just to grab a quick drink by herself and also hoping that she would see her brother Jack there since he was not answering his phone. She saw Debbie at the bar and sat down to talk to her since she had not seen her since her accident. Debbie had always known her as Richard and Jack' little sister and by the time

Debbie, Richard, and Paula were graduating college Jen was starting there as a freshman.

They caught up for a while and laughed about their horrible dating experiences over the last six months until Jack walked in. He sat down at the bar with his sister and Debbie saying sarcastically. "My favorite sister, and my favorite dike sitting here trying to make my life miserable, if that's not a cause to drink then I don't know what is."

Jen said. "I'm your only sister and your life was pretty miserable before I got here tonight."

Debbie commented before Jack could reply. "There's nothing like family to point out your shortcomings. I'll drink to that." Then she took a shot. Jack just laughed and hugged his sister.

They all got another round of drinks then started to catch up on everything in their lives except what was going on with their friends. Finally Jen changed the subject so she could tell Jack what she already knew would be hard for him to hear. She looked at her brother and said. "I need to tell you something about Sara, she's getting married again."

"I know," Jack replied.

"Well, she asked me to be one of her brides maids because she didn't have anybody else and we always got a long. I wanted to ask you first so you wouldn't be weird about it."

"I don't care, do what you want."

"Are you sure?"

"Really, its fine." Jack sighed as he finished his sentence trying to hide what he really felt. After a pause, he asked his sister. "Why do you want to do it just out of curiosity?"

"I've always liked Sara, she's like a sister to me, but if you really are going to be weird about it then I won't do it."

"It's cool, I just didn't think you were that close anymore."

"We've talked a little bit since you two split and I knew she was dating someone, but I still think it's a bit uncomfortable talking about it with you. After all you two got a divorce and you haven't said anything to each other in almost two years."

Jack laughed a little bit to himself trying to shake off the fact that he didn't want to think about it even though he had thought about Sara every day since they got a divorce. He said to Jen. "Look it's a bit weird, but if you two are still friends then great and you should help her out with that part of her wedding."

Debbie started laughing and said. "I think you're full of shit Jack, you still love her, and it bothers the hell out of you that she's getting married again not to mention that Jen is going to be in her wedding."

Jack laughed even though he knew what she said was true. He would just have to keep trying to hide his hurt, in his mind, it was working, and he was still happy. Unfortunately, we're all subject to delusions of grandeur from time to time. Jack replied to Debbie. "Believe whatever you want, but I still sleep good with out of her every night."

Jen spoke up and said. "If you want to know the truth she did ask about you and she wanted me to find out if you were going to be okay with it."

Jack got an anxious look on his face, he was glad to hear that Sara was thinking about him and Debbie saw it. Jack couldn't hide it from her. Debbie replied to Jack. "I see the look on your face, you still love her... you're happy that she's thinking about you. Why don't you just look her up and tell her how you really feel before you drink yourself to death over regret."

Jack got angry and lashed out turning the mood into something full of hate. He replied to Debbie. "Why don't you do the same and talk to Paula?" Then he looked at Jen and said. "Why don't pull your head out of your butt and talk to Jarrod." Debbie and Jen didn't know what to say, they were both surprised by his angered remarks and then Debbie replied. "Well, look at the bitch come out you."

"I'm just saying, if we're going to point out the things we're afraid to do then you two are just as guilty as I am" Jack said.

"I'm not afraid to say anything to Paula and if she were here then I could prove that to you."

"It looks like you'll get your chance because she just walked through the door."

Debbie and Jen turned around to see Paula as she walked through the door; she was alone and she looked as if she was looking for someone important to her. The three of them concluded that it had to be Richard and the bar would be a good place to find him, but he wasn't there. Jack excused himself from the table and left. As he was leaving he stopped over to say hi to Paula and told her that Richard wasn't here. When he didn't want to be found there was no way to find him until he decided to resurface. She smiled at Jack because she knew he was right and because he knew right off who she was looking for. Paula did come looking for Richard because the silence was becoming unbearable and they needed to talk, but the silence would stay a little while longer. Jack did tell her though, that there was an old friend she could talk to and pointed to Debbie.

Jack walked out the door after saying goodbye. Paula walked over to the table that Debbie and Jen were sitting at and asked if she could sit down. Debbie paused at the question for a moment, but then said yes. She knew that it was time let the anger go and put old arguments away. It's a long restless world when you don't have your best friend traveling it with you. Debbie looked at her friend and said. "I probably owe you a drink for the grief I put you through."

Paula smiled and said. "I don't know about that, maybe I owe you one for not being a better friend."

"It was never a question of that; you were always a good friend even when I was too angry to talk to everybody. My mother said you called a lot to check on me."

"I was worried...I was worried that you would never come back from this."

"I wasn't sure that I would either, but I'm here and everyday day I'm getting better. Besides I'm tired of hating everything...I'm really just tired of being angry."

Paula hugged her friend as they both shed a few tears. They were tears of sadness and they were tears of joy. Jen just looked at them and smiled then she said in kind of a sarcastic tone. "It's a beautiful thing when people can make up, it should be like this all the time for that would be a perfect day."

Paula and Debbie laughed at her comment because the sarcasm behind it was the same kind of comment that Richard would have made. That's why Paula was laughing, she missed him because whether she was ready to admit it aloud or not she needed him in her life.

Debbie looked at Paula and said. "Speaking of making up, have you had a chance to talk with Richard?" Paula said no and then looked at Jen to see if she knew where her brother was. Jen just told her that she didn't know and hadn't spoken to him in a while then she just reiterated what Jack had said to her about disappearing.

Debbie had already heard why they quit talking to each other through Jack. She was proud of her friend for telling the truth, but sad for her that she had finally met the one she always needed and this one issue would be the thing that would drive them apart. Debbie replied. "I heard that you finally told Richard the truth."

"Yes I did and I knew this would happen." Paula replied. "I'm still not sure whether it was the right thing to do, but I do know that we couldn't have made it with something like that hanging over us. I miss him and I don't know what to do."

Jen looked at Paula and said. "The only thing you can do is find my brother and make him understand. He is too stubborn when's he angry and he won't make the first step, you'll have to do it. He's too much like our dad."

"Are you sure you don't know where I can find him, he won't answer me when I go by his place." Paula asked Jen.

Jen smiled and replied. "The only thing I can tell you is, when he doesn't hang out here you can find him down at Jake's down on Clark Street. He'll probably be drunk and hitting on other women."

The answer was not what she wanted to here, but she knew that Jen was telling the truth. Debbie hugged her to try and comfort her because she knew that her friend was hurting. Debbie raised her glass, toasted with Jen and Paula to their broken hearts and misunderstood men.

As she was toasting Mina, my wife was walking around making sure the patrons in the bar were okay. She walked over to the table where the girls were sitting and started to talk to them. She was not as much of talker like me, but she liked to mingle with the guests and offer up her own simple words of female wisdom. She asked the girls. "I see you guys are in here tonight yet again without your men or woman in Debbie's case. Still having trouble with your love lives?"

Jen replied. "Were drinking to broken hearts and misunderstood men so what does that tell you?"

Mina laughed and said to her. "The broken hearts can be fixed, but men being misunderstood, it's not really true. We just make them that way because we refuse to admit the obvious. Their simple, very simple, but we like complicated men so we can fix them. That's when we're truly happy in a relationship."

All three women were surprised at her truthful answer. They were surprised that she would admit that as if she had broken some women's code where you ban together as women and never revel the secrets that you know. Also they were surprised that she would admit that women could be at fault for misunderstanding the true nature of men.

Paula asked her before anyone else at the table could. "How can you say that about men-I'm pretty sure their misunderstood. Who really knows how they're going to act, I know it's easy to say that they're always thinking about one thing and all their actions derive from that thought process, but we don't understand them just like they don't understand us."

"You really think so," Mina asked. "Men aren't always after one thing, but it's not hard to figure out what they are willing to do for us when they see that we're worth it and that's when they're more predictable."

"I don't understand," Jen said.

Mina replied. "Because as woman we tend to feel our way through life, we like the drama a bit...it may not be the case all the time, but most of the time it is. Now this may not make sense so let me ask you this, Jen you're not seeing that police officer anymore because he found out something you didn't him want to find out. He was mad that you lied to him instead of what you actually did, right?"

"I guess that's right," Jen said.

Mina said. "If you would have just told him the truth from the beginning none of this would've happened, but it comes down to the drama that we like to create."

Jen smiled at her and said. "Perhaps you have a point, but you could just be making all that up."

Mina smiled and then looked at Paula. "Now what about you and Richard, do you think he would have gotten so mad if you had told him the truth from the beginning, no, and it's not any different that when you antagonize each other just to argue or debate. You like the drama."

Paula replied to her. "He would have gotten mad if I told him in the beginning. Things would have been just as bad."

"Maybe," Mina replied. "But, the thing is it didn't even occur to you to say something then. Instead, you waited to tell him and made things worse. It doesn't matter whether it was on purpose or not, you did, and you did it for the drama."

"I don't think we're doing this to ourselves just to stir things up between us and the men in our lives." Paula said to Mina.

"Maybe or maybe not," Mina replied. "But you can't do any good by not admitting the real truth and it's what women don't like to admit. We like the complication so in the end when everything works out we know it was worth it and it makes it that fairytale type of ending. However, we can still be just as happy if we're honest from the very beginning and we don't have to go through so much."

Debbie said. "Maybe we force ourselves to go through all this shit just to make ourselves better, to make ourselves more complete so when we do have what we want in the end and we know it was worth it and we appreciate it more."

Mina smiled at her and said. "It's another way of looking at it, we don't' know what we can have until we've lost it. Remember though, we do this to ourselves and it's usually on purpose whether we want to admit it or not."

Jen asked Mina. "Does it get any easier if we know the truth behind what we do?"

"No," Mina replied. "Because then we're forced to make a choice and only by accepting our faults and the lies we tell ourselves will be able to make the hard choice. And we will have to make a hard choice in the end if we're going to be happy."

Paula asked Mina. "What choice is that?"

Mina smiled and said, "You'll know what it is when the time is right, we always know and we can't deny it."

Jen asked her. "Did you make that hard choice?"

Mina looked over at me as I was standing behind the bar helping customers. The three girls looked over in that direction. Mina said. "Yes I did and it was the one that made me truly happy." She walked off after that for there was nothing more to say. She offered her words of wisdom and left as she always did leaving those that she had spoken to, to ponder her words. It was her way and great wisdom needed to be reflected upon in order to discover the nature of it even if the wisdom came from inside a dingy bar.

Not too long after Mina left the girls left for the evening, each of them off to some other adventure. As they were leaving, they each smiled at me as if to say thank you-they knew that I had sent Mina over to give them a few words of wisdom. I was always offering some sort of advice like a father figure for lost souls who just need a little bit of encouragement. This time I figured my wife could do it better. As they smiled at me, I winked at them as if say you're welcome and also, to say that I would always be there to answer their questions and hear their cries of sorrows when all had gone wrong in their lives for that is what a father does for his children.

Paula left the bar that night with a better understanding of why everything happened the way it did with her and Richard. She had to find him and to finally set things right even if she was the one who had to swallow their pride. She was still confused and didn't know if they could get past what was between them, but she had to talk to him, that much was certain.

Late that evening she made her way to Jake's down on Clark Street. She hadn't even made her way into the bar before she saw Richard and right beside him there was a tall blonde with big tits that were clearly not real. She was all over him, touching him, rubbing on him, and grabbing things that were never meant to be touched in public even in the most erotic of circumstances. They were together outside the bar, feeling each other up and as she watched, shocked and disgusted another woman came from around the corner and joined in the fun. He never even noticed Paula; he was too engrossed with the women and the prospects of a threesome, which would happen for him later that evening.

Paula couldn't watch anymore, she quickly turned around and walked away. She tried to hide the tears from the people walking past her, but she couldn't. One of the passers on the street even commented to his friend as they walked past her that she must have caught her boyfriend cheating on her- it couldn't have been more ironic. Paula ended up home after getting a few bottles of wine -it was one of those nights for her. All she could do was have a good cry and try to figure out her life. After drinking about a half of bottle of wine she pulled out some stationary she had on her desk in the living room and sat down to write a letter. She wrote a letter to Richard, pouring her soul and her honesty on the paper and like a great writer that becomes the artist, she would bleed on those pages to Richard.

∞∞∞∞∞

That same evening Jack, who like everybody else was trying to figure things out, didn't go straight home from the bar. It was late, but not too late, so he decided to make a stop. He had to know the truth no matter how much it would hurt. He stopped by Sara's apartment on his way home. Her wedding was a few weeks away and it didn't matter to Jack, he didn't care if her fiancé was there or not, he needed know something and it was something he never had the courage to ask before.

He knocked on her door and she answered it with a sarcastic smile; she was getting ready for bed so she was in her robe. She looked at Jack and said. "The streak for bad timing continues with you."

"I'm sorry for the late hour, but I need to ask you something."

"You couldn't ask me over the phone or at a more reasonable hour?"

"I really need an answer and I couldn't wait."

She laughed and said. "I know what happens when you get that way-you can't stop thinking about it, obsessing to the point that you won't sleep. Come on in and I'll get some coffee-you look like you can use it."

"You are being awfully nice about this," Jack said sarcastically.

"Can you imagine how I would be if the divorce had been bad?"

Jack walked in and took a seat at her kitchen table while she prepared some coffee. It reminded him of the conversations they used to have when they couldn't keep silent about something. They would talk and debate something all night if that's what it took until they were both satisfied about the outcome of the subject matter. Even though they had been divorced for almost two years, they could still be friends and they could still have these conversations. For the both of them it was a comfort and it was the mark of a true friendship.

Sara looked over at Jack and asked him. "Whatever you have to ask me doesn't have to do with Jen being in my wedding."

Jack laughed because she knew how he could overreact about the little things that might not seem like a big deal. He replied. "No, that has nothing to do with it. If anything I'm glad you guys remained friends. She always liked you and saw you as a big sister."

"Well, I just wanted to make sure."

"If I said I had a problem with it, would you replace her as one of your bridesmaids?"

"No, but you already know that." Jack smiled at her sarcasm. She said to him. "I only ask because if its going to be a thing, then I won't talk about it with you."

Jack said in a more serious tone. "What I have to ask you is nothing like that."

She sat down at the table with him, handed him a cup of coffee and asked him. "So what's on your mind?"

"Why couldn't we make it, what really lead to us getting a divorce?"

"You're asking me this now... after nearly two years you're asking me this after I explained it to you more than once."

"Yeah, I'm asking now."

"You didn't listen to anything I had to say about it two years ago, did you?"

"It doesn't matter now if I did or not," Jack replied. "I'm asking you now because I need to know the truth."

"Jack, you're a piece a work. If you want to know so you can try and fix it you're a little too late."

"First of all it's never too late to do the right thing." He only told himself this even though he wasn't quite sure if it was true.

"That may be true, but you're too late with me. Now I'll answer your question if you answer something for me.

"Okay."

"Why now? Why are you doing this now? Is it because I'm getting married again and you're still alone so you have to try and make sense of it. Are you trying to find some kind of closure?"

Jack scoffed at her remarks and said. "Look I just want to know the truth. I have been thinking about things lately as everybody I know seems to be living in the warzone when it comes to their love life, and I don't care if you're getting married again."

"I know that's bullshit, you care a little bit because the reality of the divorce is finally setting in. What you're doing now is part of the problem I had with you. You think there might still a chance for you and me. You always think there's a chance, but you never do anything about it."

Jack looked at her with an angry look, the truth was starting to hurt, but he had asked for it and she was giving it to him despite how difficult it might be. He said. "I don't even know what that is supposed to mean, a chance for you and me. That chance left when we signed the papers. You're talking nonsense now."

"Nonsense, let me explain it to you in a different way, one you might understand," Sara replied. "You're stagnate and fall easily into a depressing routine despite knowing that there is a chance out there to be truly happy. We did that all through our marriage, we would fall into our routine until we didn't talk anymore and then we eventually cheated on each other. When we tried to fix everything, we were good for a while, but we fell right back into that trap. Now I'm not saying that I wasn't partly to blame, but despite the chances you had to fix everything you never did. You just let things be, hoping that they would be fixed on their own. You never dared to try and fight for us."

Jack didn't have anything good to say, but he did manage to get out "I took a chance when I asked you to marry me knowing we didn't have any money and I took a chance on us after we cheated on each other."

"Okay twice, but you let us fall into that depressing routine and you never kept taking a chance. You never kept fighting. You are the most practical man I know and it's always a bad thing, but you can't always find the success or happiness you deserve unless you're willing to take that chance and jump off the cliff."

Jack looked dumbfounded at what she said. He was hurt by it, filled with disbelief, and yet he knew she was right. Sara went on to tell him. "I'll put it to you another way. You are one of the most gifted litigators in the city of Chicago, but you never go out on a limb, sometimes bluffing your way through something just to get the right reaction out of the other guys so you how to beat them. It's like poker, you suck at it because you're never willing to bluff or go out on limb and bet on a chance. You live your life like you're trying to avoid the worst and the only way we can beat the bad stuff that happens is to just go through it fighting every step of the way if that make sense. Now I don't how many more ways I can say you have to take a chance on something, risking it anyway knowing that you might fail."

Jack gave her a half smile and said. "I didn't think you would have so much to say."

"You asked for the truth and I have a lot to say," Sara replied. "For me I need something more and maybe you didn't have it so that's why I called it quits. I hope that clears it up for you."

Jack finished his cup of coffee for there was nothing more to say. There was nothing that he could argue with her about and win. He was wrong and he knew it. She was right and he never gave enough. Perhaps he had always known that and never wanted to admit it. He got up and kissed her on the forehead. He thanked her for the cup of coffee and the truth. He said to her. "I'm sorry for everything. I really am sorry." Then Jack walked out the door.

∞∞∞∞∞

Richard woke up hung over not even knowing where he was, but the two women in the bed on either side of him reminded him. He got up, put his pants on, and then snuck out trying to forget the trudging scene that lay before him in a crumbling apartment with cocaine for decoration. It was not one of his finer moments, he thought. Half an hour later he ended up home and immediately started drinking, it was nine o'clock in the morning. For most of the day he stayed on his couch drinking beer and watching television. He didn't even bother taking a shower that day to clean off the smell of cheap beer and sex. As far as he was concerned, he did not want to remember what had happened the night before or the week before when he gone home with a married woman that he would have never dared sleep with if he had been sober and thinking straight.

At some point during the day, Paula had stopped by. She didn't knock on the door; she only slipped a letter underneath and left. She had called Debbie to let her know what she did and Debbie being a little worried about Richard called his brother Jack who then got a hold of Mike so they could do something about Richard. The two of them went over to Richard's apartment to find out what had happened to him. Mike was still not really speaking to Richard, but it didn't matter, they were still friends and Richard needed his help. He was heading down a very dark slippery slope and nobody wanted to get the call one day that the neighbors had found Richard dead after the stink from his place had become so unbearable that they were forced to call the police.

Mike still had his key so he and Jack let themselves in and they found

Richard on the couch passed out and too drunk even to remember what day it was. After a few minutes, they finally got him awake and then it took another moment for him to realize what was happening. Richard thought he had turned insane or at the very least was dreaming.

Jack laughed at his brother and said. "We're not going to let you kill yourself with alcohol tonight... you'll have to do it some other time."

Richard asked his brother. "can I do it tomorrow?"

Mike replied before Jack could say something. "If you're good tonight then we might let you kill yourself tomorrow."

Richard laughed as he slowly got himself up and off the couch. He tried to grab another beer that was sitting on the coffee table, but Jack stopped him. Jack said to him "I think you've had enough for awhile."

Richard replied. "This isn't some kind of intervention is it and by the way how did you know that I was in this state?"

Mike said to Richard. "Paula called Debbie who then called Jack and said you weren't answering your door. She also saw you last night at Jake's so she was upset."

Richard got a surprised look on his face and said. "Paula was here, I didn't hear her knock. What was she so upset about that she would call everybody?"

Jack pointed to the trashy living room filled with empty pizza boxes and beer bottles. He replied. "I think she was upset at what you were doing to yourself and when saw you last night with those two women, well, it didn't exactly make her happy. I mean look around Richard you're trying to kill yourself slowly while hoping to forget about everything that's happened to you."

"That's not true," Richard said. "Well the forgetting part might be true.."

Mike asked him. "Is the meaningless sex helping you in your mission?."

"Not really," Richard said.

"It didn't help you before either before you fell in love with Paula did it?" Mike responded back.

Richard sighed and thought about it for a moment. He then replied. "Maybe, but the sex was good even if it wasn't meaningful. I'll say this, things made a little more sense back then because they were simple."

Jack replied to his brother. "It's not supposed to be... at least that's what I've figured out."

"I know that's right," Mike said.

Jack continued to say. "All of us are perfect examples of that. I lost my marriage because I didn't take enough chances for her and now it's too late. Mike's in love with a call girl who he can't find anymore so he can make things right again even though it never should have never gotten to the point where they walked away from each other in anger. You, well, you fucked everything up with Paula because you couldn't manage any understanding with her and you would rather destroy everything about you then find forgiveness. So the three of us are one hell of a group!"

Richard didn't say anything. He just stared at his brother for a few moments. Richard finally asked his brother. "So what do we do, how do we get over it."

"I don't know," Jack replied. "I don't have any answers, just questions. The one thing I won't let you do little brother, is destroy yourself out of anger or guilt. You're better than that, we're all better than that."

Mike noticed a letter on the floor by the door. They had missed it as they walked in and it appeared that somebody had slipped under the door for Richard. Mike picked it up and noticed that it was Paula. He handed it to Richard and told him that it was from her and that she must have left it for him early that morning. Richard was surprised to see it and although he was scared to open it, knowing that what might be in it could be bad. He did open it and started reading.

Dear Richard

I still don't know what to say after everything that's happened. Sorry doesn't mean much, but you should know that I am sorry for not telling you the truth. Being in love with my boss is not even something I can explain. I never looked at it terms of right or wrong, it was something that felt good at the time. It doesn't anymore and for what it's worth being with you all those months made more sense. I was happy and that's a lot considering I used to really hate you in college You used to really annoy me, but through it all I guess I learned to really love you, to love everything about you. This may not seem much, but it's the truth. We both have things that we weren't ready to tell each other and I've learned, especially now that the truth doesn't carry much weight the longer it goes without being said. I saw you last night with those two women and it was horrifying. I'm not even mad anymore that you were with them because I finally understand. We all have our own way of dealing with the hurt and sometimes we just have to lash out, doing the things that we know are wrong. Maybe it's a form of punishing ourselves. I don't know.

I don't know if we can be together, I don't know if we could make it. It's too much uncertainty for me and the only thing I'm sure of is this, I have to go. Where I am going is somewhere only for me. It's a journey that I have to take. I wanted you to know that I was leaving. I am taking some time off and going to travel. I don't know when I'll be back or if I will ever be back, but I wanted you to know one thing. You were right. Also know this, I do love you and it's more than I've loved anybody even him. I don't want you to try and find me, just let me go. If you truly care about me, you'll let me go.

Paula

Richard wadded up the letter and threw it across the room in anger. Jack asked him what she said and he simply replied that she was leaving and he couldn't go after her because she wanted it that way. Richard didn't know what to say after that- all he wanted to do was grab another beer and crawl back in to the hole of depression he had created for himself. Mike wouldn't let him get another beer and Jack had to restrain him. Richard lashed out in anger and then he almost broke down and cried. He held the tears trying to maintain some dignity, but he couldn't hide his sorrow. The three of them sat around for some time, not really saying anything. They just watched the Cubs' game on TV.

After a while, Jack finally said that it was time for them to go and he meant all of them. He wanted to get out of the apartment and most wanted his brother to see something different in the form of scenery. He said to Mike and Richard. "Let's get out of here, this place is to depressing and I need a drink now."

"Now you're talking," Richard replied.

"Not you little brother; no more alcohol. Coffee would be a good thing for you right about now."

Richard gave him a dirty look while Mike laughed a little. Mike then said. "I think The Matador is calling. We need a place where we can laugh and have a good time."

Jack nodded in agreement and the three of them left after Richard got cleaned up. He smelled of beer and stale burritos, a fine meal for the drunken depressed. They arrived at The Matador about an hour later and found it not too busy for a Saturday night. The place still had some excitement to it, I was sarcastic as usual.

The three of them took a seat at the bar and the saddened looks upon their face could not be hidden. I walked over and said hi while getting them their usual drinks for which I had known for years, another characteristic of a great friend. When Jack told me to get coffee for Richard, I didn't argue and didn't even listen to Richard's protest. I already knew that Jack was looking out for his brother. So finally I asked Jack, Mike, and Richard. "Okay, spill it what's wrong guys, you look like you just came back from a funeral."

Jack replied. "Trinidad it's just one of those sad and lonely nights."

"So you three have women issues," I said sarcastically.

"Is it that obvious," Mike asked. "Why couldn't it be the Cubs lost and were just sad about that?"

"Because the Cubs always lose and we're used to it; besides there's not much you three can hide from me," I said as I laughed.

Jack, Richard and Mike all laughed as I smiled at them. There wasn't much they could put past me, somehow I always knew, like a guardian angel that never stops seeing the truth. Richard said to me. "You're right buddy, we're all having women issues. I know you have some advice for us."

Jack Mike and Richard just looked at me waiting for my usual words of wisdom. They were expecting something profound and humorous just like always. My advice for them, it seemed, was like a really good drug that you couldn't kick the habit from. I just looked at them and said. "I have some advice for you. It's more like a statement of fact- you guys are idiots." They were waiting for some kind of punch line thinking that I was being sarcastic, but he was very serious.

Jack asked him. "Why are we idiots?"

"Because you haven't listened to a word I've said over the years."

"What are you talking about, we've listened to you and you've always had great advice. That's one of the reasons we still keep coming here."

"But you haven't really listened-you may have heard the words, but they obviously didn't sink in or you wouldn't be sitting on a barstool feeling glum about the women that left all of you" I said with a serious tone. Nobody said anything, shocked by what I was saying. So I responded again. "I don't have any clever words of wisdom for you, nothing different from what I've said over the years and that's what makes you three the worst kind of idiot because you never really listened and here you are when you could have fixed the problems long ago."

Mike looked at me and asked."Why are you in a bad mood-I don't think we're idiots, misguided maybe, but not idiots."

"Oh Really," I said, "Everybody else agree with that?"

All three of them looked at me and said yes. I just shook his head in dismay. The he said to them. "Okay then let's really look at this for a moment. Jack do you still love Sara?"

Jack asked me. "What difference does that make?"

"It makes all the difference, answer the question or if you need help answering it then let me ask it a different way-how many women have you dated or slept with since your divorce?"

Jack looked at me and replied. "I don't think that matters either so what if I haven't been out with anybody else since then."

" So what are you waiting for get on with your life even if it's just a one night stand, lord knows you could use it."

"Maybe I don't want to, why do I need to do something like that just to prove that I might be over Sara."

"You don't have to prove it to anyone else, but yourself. However you haven't done anything like that since your divorce, which brings into question that you might be waiting for her, that you might still have feelings for her, but haven't done anything about it."

"That isn't necessarily true."

"But it's not completely undeniable either. Have you asked her since getting a divorce what really caused it and why she really left because maybe you were too curious and just had to know?"

Jack had a surprised look on his face. I was playing the psychic a little bit and the truth I knew about Jack was scaring him a little bit. Jack looked at me knowing that he couldn't lie anymore and answered. "Yes I did."

I replied. "I know you did and if you didn't really care about her or what happened between you then you wouldn't have bothered to ask her the question. You might as well admit it that you still care for her and if given another chance you would go back to her. If it's a strong love then we can't deny it or what we're willing to do if given another chance at it."

Jack sighed a bit and Richard laughed at me for the way I was acting. I looked over at Richard and said. "I wouldn't laugh quite yet, you're not much better than your brother."

Richard responded. "What did I do?"

"Plenty," I said. "Let me ask you something and it's not if you're in love with Paula-I already know that because it's written all over you face." Richard gave me a surprised look then I continued. "Richard did you ever tell Paula about your playboy ways, did you ever tell her about all the women you took back to your place and slept with? Hookers don't see as much action as you do."

"We've talked about it to a degree." Richard said.

"So that really means that you told her you weren't a virgin anymore, which she already knew, but you never told her that you would screw anything in a skirt."

"Look I never cheated on her."

"You get mad at her for not telling you the truth, but you can't be honest with her. Even when you just want to be with her you still fuck it up by sleeping around." I just stared at Richard with a cold hard look waiting for Richard to give another smart-ass remark, but Richard didn't say anything. So I said. "You can feel depressed all you want, but you could have done something about it and instead you felt sorry for yourself and wasn't man enough to step up to the plate when it came to Paula, just to give you an analogy you might understand."

Richard didn't make a comment at all. He knew I was right. There was nothing to say and even being drunk couldn't hide the truth. It stared him in the face and all he was left with now was a cold cup of coffee, a brother who was just as depressed as he was, a best friend that never had any answers about love because of all his inexperience with it, and a sarcastic bartender that wanted to make him feel worse, so it seemed.

I looked over at Mike and said. "Don't think I forgot about you. The only thing I have for are two questions. First, can you really live with her past and find forgiveness in it? Second, what are you really willing to do to be happy with her?"

Mike didn't know what to say to that, but he did muster an *I don't know*.

I replied. "At least your honest, but if you're going to have any chance with her then you 're going to have to be able to answer those two questions."

Jack said to me. "You being a little harsh tonight, you know that. Are you having problems with your wife and just taking out on us?"

I just laughed and said. "You know that's a pretty good assumption knowing how stubborn my wife is, but no. I may be a little harsh, but you need some brutal honesty tonight and sarcasm is not going to help you."

Mike looked at me and asked. "How do you know what we're really going through-did you ever go through something like this?"

"You mean was it something so bad that I was forced to make a hard choice in order to be happy

"Yes, that's what I meant?"

"The answer is yes. I can't give you advice about something that I don't know anything about."

"Well, what's your story?"
I looked the three of them with a very serious look and then looked over at my wife. Jack, Richard, and Mike looked over at her to and listened to my story while I couldn't take my eyes off Mina.

"I wasn't supposed to marry her, we weren't even from the same class of life. Her family was rich and mine wasn't. Her father didn't even like me and he told me to never see her again. We went to school together and my father was somebody that just worked for her father, making slave wages so he could barely feed his family. All of that didn't stop Mina and me, though. We loved each other and even though we were foolish people at eighteen it didn't matter. Her father wanted her to marry someone else, someone who had more prospects, more money, and in his eyes was from the right class. Her father threatened to have me killed if I ever saw her again and he had the power to do it. Night before her wedding I convinced her to run away with me and we immigrated to America to start a new life."

Jack said to me. "Sounds like to me you got the better deal."

"I did and I like to think she did to, but she gave up a lot because our lives here have never been easy. The best thing for her would have been to stay in Spain and marry the other guy. He wasn't a bad man and she would have been better off. The thing is I made a hard choice knowing that I could have been killed and I could have ruined her life... almost did. I was selfish to ask her to do all that since it was not the best thing for her, but we've made it work. The other issue is I took her away from her family and she never saw them again. It's a hard choice to make when asking the woman you love to abandon all that, it's a hard choice to make when you know that the smart thing is not ask them to gamble on their happiness. I did it because I thought I could make it work and I have to a point, but there is a lot that she will never get back and a lot that I put her through all just for my own selfish gain. But the hardest choice to make is to stay with it and to keep working hard every day to make them happy because they're worth it. Ask yourselves, can you really do that?"

Richard looked at me and said. "I still don't get it, it seems like she made more of a hard choice than you did."

"You know how difficult my wife is, you have to make a hard choice to put up with that," I said in jest. "The truth is the only way you can understand about making a hard choice is to finally do it. Only then will you finally understand."

Richard said. "At least tell me this, was it worth it?"

I just looked at him with a smile on his face "I'm still with her and I'm telling a story that has nothing to do with regret. This is not some sad story where everything didn't work out so what do you think?"

Richard just smiled at me. The light bulb was finally turning on and so it finally did for Jack and Mike as well. They got what they really came for, it was harsh and it was brutal, but it was worth it. I looked at all three of them and said "Okay, now I have one more piece of advice that's not quite so harsh and if you listen to anything I tell you this is what you should remember. You want to change your life and really be happy especially when faced with making that hard choice. Courage has nothing to do because we're willing to try or do anything when we're desperate enough. You have to be good and strong. You have to want to be better than what you are. You have to be strong enough to keep fighting through all the shit that comes your way so in the end you're still standing. You have to be willing to go through all that in order to be happy. This may not make much sense, but it will when you're ready to do it. And that is all I have to tell you."

So after all that I walked off to help other customers leaving Jack, Mike, and Richard to think about what had been said. They all just sat there pondering my words and for the first time since everything had happened they figured what they had to do to win the Sex Game. Now the only question was would they do it, but we all know that happy endings are only reserved for Hollywood.

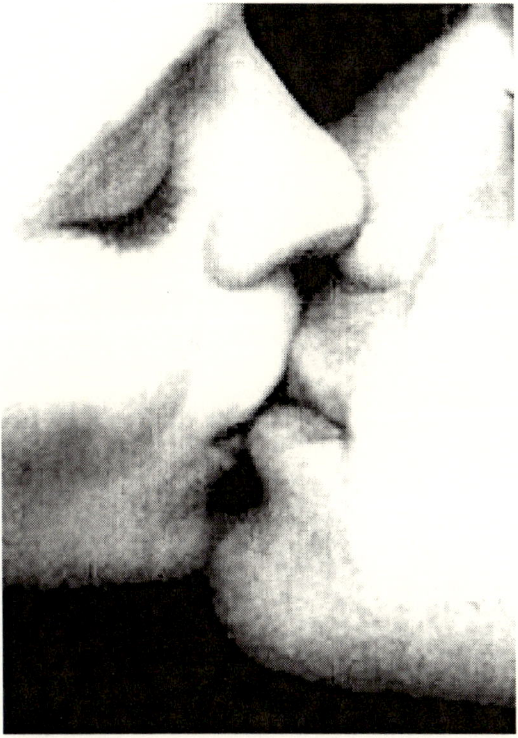

8

The Ending We Choose to Make

The rest of this story is not Trinidad's to tell. It's our story and the story can only be told by the characters living it every day. Now we each have our own version and sometimes all those versions of the story fade into one story. Our story involves all of us and not just certain individuals. The rest of this story is, well, everybody's story because we've all gone through something like this before and we've all been forced to make some hard choices. So if the tone changes just a little bit then we apologize now, for we are not as good as Trinidad when it comes to telling this story.

∞∞∞∞∞

     Jack lay on the church pew holding an ice pack to the side of his face; he laid there staring up at the ceiling glad that the bleeding had stopped from his nose while bloody tissue paper was stuck up his nostrils. It was not one of his finer moments and all he could do was think about the embarrassment of what he had done and also the embarrassment he had caused for Sara while people were walking past his pew snickering at him. He had certainly caused a commotion at the church that day and still hadn't figured out whether it was a good thing or a bad thing. Now this might be the perfect setting for a tragic ending, but the story doesn't stop here, nor does it start here. It starts right where we had left off. There are quite a few interesting satirical moments that got everybody to this place. A church might seem like a perfect haven from the trouble that we bring upon ourselves. For this little band of characters who trudge too cautiously through life this particular church is just one more comical place where honesty and bad timing render its comedic nature.

It had been a few weeks since Trinidad and Mina had offered their advice to everyone and to be quite honest during the course of those weeks there wasn't a soul who didn't ponder their words carefully. Nobody really did anything about their problems, but even though you can ignore them for a while eventually they come knocking. Now this has been said before, but its never been more true until these particular two weeks of everybody's lives came to be. Like a domino effect it started with one little thing.

      Richard was the first one to change. He had quit drinking, he dried out a little bit while starting to exercise more , and he looked closely at what his life had become. I don't think he had ever realized before how much of a mess he was, he was too drunk most of the time to take notice. Richard started to become a better person, he started helping people more, and he offered his tutoring services teaching under privileged kids how to write a couple nights of week. It might have been just something to do for a few weeks until he got bored, but at least he was trying. Richard had to start somewhere and everyday he was trying to be better. He was even more polite to people instead of being the usual sarcastic asshole that he could sometimes be.

The next the big thing to happen was with Jen and Jarrod. They hadn't spoken to each other for over six months and each of them had tried to get on with their lives by going on dates with other people. It didn't work out with the other people, but they were trying to get on with their lives. As it so happened somehow by accident they would end up back in each other's lives.

One day, out of the blue, Jen got a call from a hospital in the middle of the night about Jarrod. She was still his emergency contact and he had, had an accident while on duty. He had broken his foot while in pursuit of a burglar and he needed somebody to take him home as well as stay with him since he couldn't move around. Jen still didn't know why she was called, or if it really was an accident, but she went to the hospital anyway. She arrived not too long after the call and Jarrod was just as surprised to see her, as she was to be there.

He looked at her with a surprised look when she entered the room and said to her. "What are you doing here, you're the last person I would expect to see her."

She said to him "That's kind of funny considering I'm still your emergency contact."

"Really," he said while laughing. "I guess I never got around to changing that. You don't have to do anything. I'll get one of the guys to take me home."

"And who is going to look after you since you can't move for while."

"My sister can help me."

"Please your sister is so neurotic that she freaks out over boiling water. Yeah your sister really is the best choice to help you."

"She's not that bad."

Jen looked at him with a sarcastic look and just stared at him until he said something. Jarrod said to her. "Okay, maybe she is that bad, but I'm sure it will be fine as long as she's not in the kitchen."

"Right, as much as I don't like you these days I would be a very bad person if I let you go through something like that when I could have prevented it."

"So what are you saying?"

Jen smiled as she walked over to the where his things were in the chair and she folded them properly. Then she replied, "I'm saying that I'll be the one taking care of you until you can move around better. I'm not still mad at you and we're going to get back together, but I am going to help you."

Jarrod smiled at her and said. "Whatever you say."

Jen helped Jarrod back to his place and she took a few weeks off so she could stay with him and help him recover. The fact is they were both still crazy about each other and they weren't going to just stop what might end up being a good thing. Even though they didn't want to say it they wanted to be with each other so they just picked up where they had left off. They got over what they were fighting about, but only after they had a few long talks about what they really wanted from each other. Jarrod was laid up for two weeks before he could move again and Jen was taking care of him, what else were they going to do?

Now they could have ignored the real issue between them, but they made a choice, they chose to work it out and they were willing to fight for it even if they were forced into it a little bit. Accidents happen all the time and you have to ask yourself, what if Jarrod had never gotten hurt, what if Jen had not been listed as his emergency contact. And what if she had never come. Sometimes we make choices that we don't realize will have the best outcome for us. Sometimes we make the hard choice that works out for the best, but there are never guarantees. Sometimes it doesn't work out, but it's a gamble we have to take and if we never take it then we'll never know it when it does work out in our favor.

  So that was it with Jen and Jarrod, they did get back together despite that fact that they could really annoy each other to the point of madness and being together constantly for two weeks will definitely do that for two people. However, you also find out something you didn't know, you might really care about them more than you know and could never admit. After that Jen and Jarrod were rarely apart and somehow, as crazy as it sounds, they just knew that there wasn't anybody else for them. Two weeks is all it took for them to find that out. They wanted to be with each other and just needed the catalyst to bring them back into each other's lives. Jen was the right person for Jarrod and Jarrod was the right person for Jen; they knew it couldn't be any better that. At least if you ask them, that's what they'll say.

  The next week Richard and Jack met for their usual weekly breakfast at their favorite diner. They were both still thinking hard about what I had said and its part of what they discussed over breakfast. Richard told his brother what he had been doing about getting his life straight. Jack smiled and laughed, but in a good way towards his brother for having the courage to admit that he was a mess. He asked Richard. "So did you try and find Paula, I know you went by her place to try and catch her before she left."

"If you already know then why are you asking me?"

"I just want to hear you admit."

"Of course I went by, but I was too late. She was already gone and she had sublet her apartment. I think the people there are already annoyed at me for checking up on her."

Jack rolled his eyes at his brother and said to him." You're an idiot, you know that? You don't have to go by everyday and bother those people trying to find out if there's any news about Paula. They're not going to know anyway. You want to find out something then ask Debbie?"

"First of all I didn't go by every day, just ever other day. Second, I don't think Debbie would actually tell me."

"Probably not, but obsessing about it is not going to get you anywhere either."

"I'm not obsessing about it, I just want to set things right. I just want to talk to her and besides at least I have the guts to go after her and try to make things right.."

Jack gave Richard a dirty look and said. "I don't even know what that's supposed to mean."

"You know what that means."

"I really don't, would you care to explain it to me?"

"Have you actually talked to Sara about her getting married?"

"Why would I do that?"

"Because you don't want her to get married, you still love her and you won't go after her."

"What is there to go after, we're divorced. It's too late for that."

"No its not, you're still fair game until you say 'I do.' You still have a few days and we both know that there's nobody else you want to be with. There's nobody else you could be with."

"I appreciate the pep talk, but it's too late."

Richard just looked at him with a disappointed look. He didn't say anything to his brother for a moment. He didn't have anything to say. Jack finally asked him, "what, you don't have any clever remarks for me because you seem to have all the answers?"

"No I don't, there are no answers I can give because if you can't see the obvious then I can't help you." Richard pulled out a ten-dollar bill and set it on the napkin dispenser. "I'll bet you ten dollars that you will never have the guts to go after the woman you truly love."

"I'm not betting you anything."

"Then I already win. This is part of what Trinidad called the *Sex Game* that we shouldn't fuck up. I know I'm not going to, I'm going to keep trying everyday because I think that's what it's about. You should do the same...but what do I know."

Richard got up and started walking out. Jack shouted," This is ridiculous, sit down and we can talk about something else. You don't have to storm out like a little brat." Richard turned around and said to his brother. "You know what's ridiculous, even now you know what the right answer is and you'll still go the other way because you're too damn scared. I'm scared too, but I'd whether try than never try at all." With that said Richard walked out and left Jack sitting there confused and angry.

Over the next few days, Jack didn't think about anything else. He kept asking the questions, *what if Richard's right* and *what if Sara would really take him back*. All he had were questions of *what if*. He did everything he could to try and solve his problem. He looked at the pros and cons; he even called his father for advice, which he hadn't done in ten years. All his father could say was that no matter what, it would still be a hard choice and he would have to live with it. The night before the wedding, he went home and opened a bottle of good scotch. He sat in his favorite chair thinking about it throughout the night and still had no answer. Although he really did have the answer, but Jack still wasn't ready to admit aloud what he really wanted to do. Maybe it was fear, maybe he figured he still had time even though he always said it was too late, or maybe the right moment hadn't presented itself yet. Jack eventually fell asleep in his chair with no answers, just more questions.

    That's the way it goes sometimes, all we have are questions and no answers because there are no perfect answers. Sometimes the answer that we do know doesn't become clear until the last possible moment. It's that moment when more time doesn't exist and we are finally forced to make that hard choice, for bad or for worse we have to make that hard choice. Sometimes procrastination can be our downfall instead of prudence. And sometimes we let the moment, the chance slip away into the dark of our own tormented soul because having courage is too hard, but our own guilt and long memory serves as the driving knife in the fading existence of what we used to be.

Jack knew all of this, so did Richard, Mike, Paula, Debbie, Jen, Jarrod, Nicole, and even Sara. Where some were ready to make a choice that could lead them to happiness or their own despair Jack teetered on the edge waiting to see what the outcome might be, but there is no outcome without action. By Saturday morning, the day of Sara's wedding, there was an answer and it was the only conclusion Jack could come up with. It had been there all along, waiting for him to admit it.

Jack got up and put the bottle of scotch away. He showered and shaved and he got dressed for one of the most important days of his life. He called his sister Jen and asked her where the church was?

Jen replied "Jack why do you want to know, you're not going to make a scene are you?"

"I have no guarantees about that, but I need to know."

"Why do you need to know this bad?"

"Because I have say my peace before it's too late."

"Jack, I love you, but this is not the time to make a mess of things."

"Maybe it's the right time. Maybe I've been waiting for the last ten years for the right time, that's why it's taken me so long. Now are you going to tell me or not?"

Jen was still reluctant to tell him, but she finally did and then told Jack not to cause too many problems even though it didn't make a difference what she said. Whatever happened was going to happen and at this point nothing could stop that. The next phone call Jack made was to his brother Richard. Richard answered with a depressed tone. He didn't want to have another long conversation about *what ifs* and I could have done this or that. Before Richard could say anything else Jack said. "Richard...you owe me ten dollars."

Richard's tone immediately changed and he got excited. He said to his brother. "It's about time you came around, little late, but better than never."

"Well come pick me up, if I'm going to embarrass myself like a crazy person then I'm not doing it alone."

"I'll be there in 15 minutes."

Richard did just like he said, he was there in 15 minutes and Mike was with him as well, for moral support of course. Jack wasn't too surprised. Jack looked at them when he got in the car and started laughing. He said, "I guess all we need now is Debbie to make it a party."

Richard said. "I already called her; she'll meet us at the church. Call her and tell her where." Jack grabbed the cell phone from Mike who was sitting in the backseat and called Debbie. He didn't really want a spectacle at the church, but when you're going to cause a mess that could land you in some trouble you always want your friends there with you. Debbie met them at the church and her first question was did Jack have a plan.

Jack shook his head no and then asked Debbie. "Do I really need one? I was just going to go in there and find her so I could talk to her."

Richard looked at his brother and said. "That's a good plan, but I think the wedding has already started."

Jack said. "Shit …what now?"

"How should I know, I've never stopped a wedding before."

"What about that girl a few years ago, Margot. Wasn't that her name?"

"I only slept with her the night before the wedding and she changed her mind on her own, totally not the same thing as this."

Debbie looked at Jack and said. "Just go in there and say *objection*-you're good at that. Then say I object to this wedding, after that just tell Sara what you have to say."

Mike said in sarcastic tone. "Before you do that we should play the song *Mrs. Robinson* just for inspiration."

Richard and Debbie started laughing and Jack just gave him a dirty look. Then he said sarcastically "Thank you Dustin Hoffman."

They got to the church and before Richard could completely park the car Jack got out and ran into the church as the ceremony was starting. Sara and her fiancé were in the middle of their vows. Jack just stood there in the back of the church without anybody taking notice while Debbie, Mike and Richard took a seat in one of the back pews. Jack paused for a moment and then Debbie kicked him hard in the ass to get him to say something. Finally, Jack with all the courage he could muster shouted aloud. "I object...I object to this whole thing."

Everybody in the church turned around to see who said it. Jen saw her brother and started shaking her head in disbelief and under breath where only the bride and her bridesmaids could hear, "Oh shit, here we go."

Sara looked at Jack with complete shock and as Jack started walking towards her, she said to him. "Jack for god sake what are you doing?"

"I don't want you to get married without me saying something first."

"You've got be kidding me...now...you think now is a good time to talk about this."

"If not now then it'll be too late."

The groom looked over at Sara and asked her, "who the hell is this guy?"

Sara answered him by saying in a somewhat angry tone "he's my ex-husband."

The Groom looked at her and then he looked at Jack and said. "You got a lot of balls showing up here and trying to ruin my wedding."

Jack looked at him and said, "I'm sorry, I'm not trying to ruin anything for you, but if I don't tell Sara now what I have to say then I never will and I can't live with that."

Sara shook her head in disbelief and said to Jack. "This is really not the time, you had your chance a few weeks ago when you came over late that night." The groom gave Sara an angry look as if she was some cheating harlot who had nothing but betrayal and contempt for him. He tried to say something, but Sara cut him off and said. "I'll handle this." Then she looked at Jack and said. "Can't you write it in a letter and send it to me later."

The minister took a seat behind the pulpit so the bride and her ex-husband could finish. He had seen many strange things in 30 years of ministry, but nothing quite like this. Who would have thought an ex-husband would stop a wedding, but when you're a man of God strange circumstances tend to go with the territory. He knew well enough to just let them handle their issues right then and there because a church is the perfect place for penance and redemption wrapped up with a little irony.

Jack looked at Sara with a serious and heartfelt look and said. "I can't just do this in a letter; I have to do this face to face. You were right about me."

"I was right about what," Sara asked him.

"I never took a chance with you and I never fought for us hard enough. You were right to divorce me. Hell I wouldn't want to live with that. I was so wrapped up in my career and my own wants that I couldn't see that. I couldn't even see how devastating it was when I had an affair."

Sara smiled and replied. "I'm glad that you can admit that now...I'm glad that you were listening. During our ten years of marriage I never thought you were listening."

"I was listening to a point, but I only heard what I wanted to hear though."

"Look Jack, I'm glad that you finally realized all of this now, but what do you really want."

"I want you, I've always have."

"And you have to tell me this now, when I'm getting married again. You couldn't do this before."

Jack smiled at her and said. "That doesn't matter, at least it shouldn't. You always said I never took that chance when it really counted, well I'm here now and telling you that I love you and that I don't want to spend the rest of my life with anybody else. I want you...I need you."

"What if I don't want you?"

"If that's the way it has to be, okay, but is that really true?"

"I'm getting married, that doesn't tell you something?"

"You still haven't answered my question."

"You should already know the answer to that question."

Jack walked up to her and said. "The only thing I know is this. You can marry him today and you might be happy with him. I can go on with my life, and probably be happy too, but I know what we used to be and I know what we can be again. I'm here taking a chance on you and me. Can you honestly tell me that you haven't thought about that or what could happen if I showed up like this and really took a chance on us?"

Sara stared at him in her beautiful white dress. She didn't know what to say because she never thought this would happen. The truth is she still loved Jack and always did. He was perfect for her. She was at her best when she was with him and he was at his best when he was with her. Sara couldn't deny that. She smiled at Jack and as the groom looked over at her she started to say something, but the groom cut her off.

He said to Jack. "Enough of this shit, I'll give you something to think about." He leaned over and blindsided Jack with a right hook; it caught Jack on the side of his eye and cut him open. Then the groom started taking shots at him beating him senseless before Jack could really defend himself. That's when an all out fight broke out in the church, Richard and Mike ran up front to defend Jack, Richard even got a few shots in on the groom before he was blindsided by one of the groomsmen. Jarrod who was sitting in the front row because of his foot got up and hopped on one foot trying to break up the fight. Jarrod in the course of trying to break up the fight did get a few shots in on the groom and his best man who were trying to kick the shit out of Jack. Jack was already on the ground with a few cuts and a broken nose. He was bleeding pretty badly.

It took a few minutes for the fight to be broken up and for Jack to be helped over to a pew so he could lie down and they could try to stop his bleeding. The church was cleared and the wedding was officially stopped. Because of the fight the bride and groom were not allowed to have a wedding there now, not that it made much of a difference at this point. Jen finally got an icepack and some towels to help stop Jack's bleeding. There was quite a bit of commotion with the wedding guests, the grooms family were irate over the situation even though it was the groom who started the fight.

    Finally, everybody was out of the church except Richard, Mike, Debbie, Jen and Jarrod. So, there was Jack staring up at the ceiling with a bloody face and a broken nose. He had taken a serious beating and wasn't sure whether he didn't deserve it or not for all the years that he had let things slip away with him and Sara.. In some small way he had to go through something like this to finally be free, free of his own guilt and fear like we all get sometimes when it comes to love. Sara came walking in and asked if she could be alone with Jack for a moment. The rest of the gang cleared the room. Jen as she was walking out past Sara looked at her and said. "Remember he's a stubborn ass, you can't really blame him for what he does?" Sara and Jen smiled at each other in amusement.

    Sara took a seat by Jack as he sat up hoping that the bleeding had stopped. She looked at him with a serious look trying not to laugh at him and at the way he looked. It was funny in a way, if nothing else because of what he went through to get to this point. She said to Jack. "You're a real son of a bitch, you know that."

"Yeah I do and I'm sorry for today, but I had to take a chance."

"I see that, your timing is still pretty bad."

"I'm sorry, I just didn't want you to be married without knowing how I felt."

Sara smiled at him. Then she rested her hand on his. She said "Jack I'm always going to love you. You're my first love, but I don't know if we can work again. I'm not going to marry you again."

"Sara I'm not asking you to, I just don't want you to be married to anybody else."

"That's pretty selfish of you, thank you for telling me that."

Jack laughed at her and then he said. "It's not like that, really. I don't want you to be married because I want to take you on a date, a real date."

Sara rolled her eyes and smiled at Jack. "I already know what your dates are like and I'm not interested in the same old routine."

"I'm not that guy anymore."

"Really, you've changed that much."

"What do you think; I just showed up and ruined your wedding while pledging my undying love for you without having changed a little bit"

"You have a point, but I still don't know about this."

"And the only way you will is to take a chance and go out with me."

Sara laughed at Jack; it was amusing that he would use her words against her. She replied, "I'll think about it, but I have to go straighten out your mess. You really out did yourself today."

"Does this mean you won't be getting married?"

"I'm not going to tell you that, except to say, you've given me something to think about-I never would have thought my fiancé would start a fight in a church. I guess I have you to thank for that."

Jack smiled at her as she got up to walk out of the church. He said to her, "Anything I could do to help you honey." He hadn't called her that since before they had cheated on each other. Sara smiled at him; it was smile that she hadn't given him in years. "By the way," he said to her, "you look amazing in that dress."

Sara kept her smile when looking at him again and said "Why don't you call me tomorrow. Also you should go to the hospital, you might need stitches."

That was it, she walked out of the church and Jack was smiling as the whole gang walked back in to see if he was all right. Jen looked at her brother, smiling then she said. "I told you not to cause a mess with the wedding-I'm glad you didn't listen to me. Looks like Sara's fiancé is a real asshole."

Jack laughed and said. "Yeah I have his kind of love written all over my face."

"Speaking of your face," Richard said. "I think it's time you go to the hospital. You're probably going to need stitches." He helped Jack up and they all walked out of the church together except for Jarrod who hobbled a long. He said to Jen "You know you have a crazy family; I've never seen something like this before."

She said. "With friends and family like this, you never have a dull moment and who really wants that anyway." Everybody just laughed as they all walked out of the church. They were a rag tag group of tormented and comical people whose lives were anything but dull-that's what made them great. That's the way it was supposed to be for only in the end do we truly know anything worth knowing having gone through some kind of satirical tragedy that we usually bring upon ourselves. There is always more truth in satire and tragedy- they are the mirror for us to see who we really are.

∞∞∞∞∞∞

    Jack was taken to the hospital and as it turned out, he did need stitches for some of his cuts. His nose had to be reset since it was broken in two places-that doesn't really seem possible, but that's what the doctor said. He even went on to say, that he had never seen a break like that before to which Jack replied. "That's because you've never met somebody like me or my friends and family-we have a unique sense of bad luck."
    The doctor laughed and he could see what a strange bunch we really were, but also how much everybody cared about each other. We did care about each other because when you go through something like we all did, you learn to rely on each other to get through the bad times. You can't help but care for one another; even

learn to love one another for that's what happens when you have great friends.

Later in the evening while Jack was still waiting to be discharged by the doctor He got a surprise visitor. Everybody was hanging around the waiting area when she walked in the doors of the hospital, it was Sara. Everybody looked at her, shocked that we would have shown up that night, but she did. She told the nurse that she was Jack's wife even though it was a little bit of a lie so she could get inside the treatment area to see him. Jack was surprised to see her although his eyes lit up when she walked in. He asked her why she was here.

Sara responded by saying, "Can't you figured it out. I still care about you and I wanted to make sure you were going to be okay. You were right about me and I thought I should be the one to take you home.."

Jack smiled for there was nothing to say, she had said it all and he didn't have to tell her what she already knew. She stayed with him until he got discharged from the hospital and then she took him home. Nobody else volunteered because as far as they were concerned Sara was the right person to take him home. The story behind Jack and Sara did have an ending. It's not the one you might think, but it did have an ending.

A week later they went on a date together and it was not the usual date that they had once had. Jack took Sara to a place that she had never been before, it was a place that he'd never wanted to go to and in his own selfishness he had never taken Sara. He took her to the opera; it was La Boehme by Puccini and so it started from there. Slowly, day by day, they reconnected and they started over, becoming in a relationship what they should have always been.

Six months later, when they were living together again, but that was only the official date after he stopped her wedding. The truth is she took him home that night and never really left. She spent most of her nights at their old apartment with him, which led to them living together again. They found out some other news six months later, Sara was pregnant with their first child. It was a surprise for both of them, but unlike before, it wasn't anything that would destroy them as couple. They actually grew stronger as a couple and they made it work. In truth, they were excited and their outlooks about life changed, but only for the better. Jack and Sara never really got married again, they never had a ceremony or renewed their vows. They just went on with their lives and started to live up their original vows. They had been through their ups and downs when it came to their relationship and they survived. Now they were just going on with their lives, together, and as a family. This would be their greatest victory and its what made them find their happiness again.

∞∞∞∞∞

    As everybody was leaving the hospital, something caught Richard's eye. It was somebody familiar, somebody that had affected both his and Mike's life in a strange way, but for different reasons. He noticed one of the nurses that had come on duty for the night shift. It was Nicole and Mike didn't notice her at the time, but Richard did and it was only right that he would be the one to notice her. In his mind, he was the only one that could make it right because it was his fault for what happened between Mike and Nicole. He constantly thought to himself, if only he had not gone to that party, if only she had not been working that night, none of this would have happened. However, *what ifs* never solve anything, they torment us until we can't see clearly and we don't know anymore what the real problem is.

Richard ignored the *what ifs* and walked up to her. She was surprised to see him, but she did say hi. Richard smiled and asked how she was doing and how the new job was going. It was obvious she had finally succeeded in getting her nursing license so she could finally change careers.

After they talked briefly, Nicole asked him. "So what did you want?"

"I wanted tell you that I was sorry for what happened and that it was my fault for what happened between you and Mike."

"It wasn't all your fault, we had something to do with it."

"Maybe you're right, but I was a cause and I want to make it right."

Nicole smiled at him and replied. "There's nothing you can do, it's already been done."

"I disagree. Mike really, really likes you. I've never seen him happier than when he was with you. You brought that out in him."

"Is that really true?"

"Yes, and I have the feeling that you really like him too. Be honest, he made a difference in your life because he didn't see you as just an escort."

She smiled because Richard was right and she couldn't really hide it. Nicole said. "You're not wrong, but I don't how we can start over and forget everything that's happened."

"Maybe you can't, but it's worth finding out, don't you think?"

"What do you want from me," Nicole said in a sad tone. "What do you want me to say, that you're right and I should forgive and forget. It's not that easy."

"Nobody said it would be. All I want is for the both of you to give it another shot."

"To be honest I don't know if I can do that."

"To be honest I don't know if he can either, but try anyway. Next week we're all getting together at The Matador for dinner and drinks, just like old times. Stop by and you two can decide from there. He's worth it and I have a feeling that you're worth it too. You won't know unless you give it a shot."

Richard wrote down the time and the date on his business card and handed it to her. He looked at her one more time before leaving and said. "Just try and go from there." She smiled at him as he turned around to leave. That was it, Richard did the best thing he could do for his friend and the woman he loved. He took the blame for their hurts and he gave them the opportunity to make things right by humbling himself to admit that he was wrong and he tried to bring them together.

∞∞∞∞∞

A week later, everybody met at The Matador on Saturday night for drinks and dinner. There was Jack and Sara, Jen and Jarrod, Debbie and her girlfriend Ashley, Mike, and Richard. Debbie and Ashley had started to see other a few months before, she was the on-call nurse the night Debbie was brought in as a rape victim. It turned out she was the best thing for Debbie. She made it easier for Debbie to get past the tragedy that had happened to her. She was an important part of the healing process for Debbie. Somewhere they found more than just an attraction between them, but a passion that would make each of them whole. They found each other and a love grew from there.

Of course, there were a couple people missing, but that soon changed. Nicole did show up not too long after everybody else arrived. Richard smiled at her as she walked in the door. Mike looked up to see what Richard was smiling at and it was a big surprise when he saw her. He couldn't believe it and he knew that Richard had something to do with it. Mike got up and walked towards her.

He asked her. "What are you doing here?"

"I don't know exactly," she replied. "Your friend Richard invited me."

Mike smiled and said, "He did uh."

"Yes he did, but if you don't want to see me after the way we left things I understand."

"I was an idiot, I shouldn't have said what I said to you or did what did. I guess what I'm really saying is I was wrong."

"We both said things –it's not entirely your fault."

"If I had done what I should have done then we wouldn't be here."

Nicole smiled at Mike, laughing a little bit at his apology or his attempt at one. Then Nicole replied, "I don't think any of that matters now, it only matters what we do now."

"In that case, I don't want to quit seeing you. I want to be with you and if there's a second chance I'll fight for it. "

"Are you sure, you know my past."

"Yes, I do, but if Captain Malcolm Reynolds can still love Anora despite her being a companion then the rest of this doesn't matter."

Nicole laughed at the sci-fi reference-it was a cheesy and goofy thing to say, but that's what she liked about him. Most people might be mad at a reference where a guy loves a classy whore, but in her own strange way, she found it charming. Nicole replied. "Nice reference."

"Somehow I knew you would like it. Look I want to try this again, can we start over?

Nicole didn't know what to say she still had her doubts because; who would really want her with the kind of past she had. Mike was the only one who did – it took him a while to settle that one issue, but he did. For the first time in his life, he knew what he wanted and he didn't care about the past or what anybody might think. She wanted him too and although she wasn't entirely convinced that Mike could live with her past transgressions she had faith, she wanted to believe that he could live with them and for now that was enough. Nicole looked at Mike with the most heartfelt look she had ever had for him. She said. "Okay, let's do it-why don't you start with introducing me to your friends."

Mike and Nicole walked over and he introduced her to everybody. He said "Everybody this is Nicole, the woman I'm absolutely crazy about." She hugged him and smiled at the comment he made. Everybody around the table introduced themselves and welcomed her as one of their own. Mike looked over at Richard and asked him. "Did you have something to do with this?"

Richard smiled and replied. "Every once in a while I can do a nice thing for someone."

"Thank You."

"I figured it was time I be a nice guy," Richard said while laughing just a little bit. He gave his goofy sarcastic smile where he trying to be suave. It was kind of charming, because in reality Richard was not that suave.

Nicole fitted right into the group of friends and family. It was as if she had always been apart of Mike's life. Jack motioned the waitress over to see if Trinidad was about. Nobody had seen him when they all walked in and they wanted to tell Trinidad what had happened with all of them. Jack asked her. "Is Trinidad around, we didn't see him when we walked in.

She replied. "Who are you looking for?"

"Trinidad, the owner of the place."

"There's nobody by that name here and the owner of the bar is named James."

"What are you talking about. You're not new here are you?"

"No, I've been working here for a few months now."

"Well, you got to know Trinidad."

"Afraid not, There's no one here by that name and I would remember if there was with a name like that."

Jack gave her a strange look. Everybody else was surprised as well. At first, they all thought that Trinidad might be playing a joke on them, but as it turned out there was no joke about it. Richard and Jack went to the bar to talk to the manager and see what was going on. He confirmed it, there was no one named Trinidad that had ever worked there and the owner of the bar who had owned the place for thirty years didn't look like Trinidad at all. He wasn't even Spanish. They asked about Mina and got the same answer-there had never been anybody by that name either. Richard saw some of the regulars in the bar and he went around asking them about Trinidad. Everybody looked at Richard as if he was crazy, nobody had ever heard of Trinidad or remembered a Spanish man working there. The regulars that had been coming to the bar for as long as Jack and Richard never remembered Trinidad or Mina.

    It was weird, it was as if he had never existed and the only people that knew of Trinidad were Jack, Richard, Jen, Jarrod, Debbie, Paula, Debbie, Nicole and Sara. Everybody at the table was surprised and didn't know what to make it. Each of them had their own very clear and distinctive memory of Trinidad and Mina. The memories seemed very real, but still nobody had ever heard of Trinidad. It left them all wondering who they had been talking to over the years at The Matador.

    After while the owner of bar, James Hilton, came by the table and introduced himself. He said that he had never heard of the person everybody was looking for, but he remembered each of their faces like he did with most of the regulars. He wanted to introduce himself and clear up any misunderstanding, so he told everybody. Finally, he pulled out of his pocket a letter that had been delivered to his bar a few weeks before. It had attention to Jack and the gang written on it.

James went on to explain that he didn't know what to do with it, but kept it just in case it was for a customer. When heard the names Jack and Richard he knew that the letter must have been for them as well as the rest of their friends. He pulled it out of his pocket and gave it to Jack then he walked off. Jack opened the letter and it had just a few lines.

To our young friends

Accidents happen all the time to which we can never control. It doesn't matter however, what matters is what we choose to believe and what we choose to act upon. That's the only thing you have to know to find joy and success in life.

Trinidad and Mina

Jack smiled and passed the letter around so everybody could see it. They all just smiled after reading it because it was true and whether Trinidad and Mina were real, it was just like them to pass along such simple and truthful words. Nobody ever figured out what really happened with Trinidad or Mina and whether they were real or not, but they all talked about them as if they were so I guess they were real in some way. They talked about them as if they were the best of friends or a member of their own family. They remembered Trinidad and Mina as teachers whose wisdom was sometimes better than that of their own parents. The only sad note was that Paula wasn't there with everybody, but that didn't matter either because she was with them in the stories they all told of one another. The gang sat at their favorite place, drinking, eating, and just being happy. For some their story was a happy one and it all worked out in the end. They made the hard choices and it was worth it. However, stories like this don't always end on a happy note and that's also the way it supposed to be.

∞∞∞∞∞∞

About six months later just as Jack and Sara were finding out they were having a baby they all found out some really bad news. For the last six months everything was great. Everyone was happy and the relationships between them were the best they had ever been. Mike and Nicole were living together now and their lives were as if she had never had a past and they didn't meet under such strange circumstances. Jen and Jarrod were six months pregnant. Apparently, the two weeks they spent together while his foot was broken turned out to be really good for them and with a little surprise on the way. It became more evident that they had grown closer. They even had a little wedding ceremony a few months later, nothing too big. Jen and Jarrod getting married wasn't really a surprise-the baby was, but not really. It was bound to happen.

Debbie and Ashley were doing good and as it turned out Ashley was the woman Debbie had always been looking for even when she was flirting with young guys at the bar. Who knew that a tragedy could bring people together by and that accidental circumstance would be the best thing in the world for two lonely people. Richard, well, he was also doing good. He was happy and had become a better person. He wasn't lonely as one might think, but he did miss Paula. He missed her and he had hope that one day she would return having found what she had always been looking for in herself.

It wasn't to be however. One night Debbie got a call from Paula's mother letting her know that Paula had been killed in a plane crash on her way back to England. She had taken a small private airline from Iceland, the plane was flying in bad weather and it went down over the Norwegian Sea. After a week's search, the plane and the bodies were found. It was a freak accident, rescue workers from Norway said, one of those things that never happens except one out of a million times when a plane crosses the Norwegian Sea. It just so happened, that Paula was on that plane with a million to one chance.

Debbie was shocked and it was hard to tell the others especially Richard. Paula was finally coming home after being gone most of the year. She was also a different person, according to her mother, a better person. The trip had done her a world of good, but that doesn't stop tragedy from happening. It's unfair, it doesn't always make sense, it just happens. Everybody was devastated over what happened with Paula, especially Richard and for a while, he became again, what he used to be.

    It would be a couple of weeks before her body could be brought back to the states and in those two weeks while everyone went through their own grieving process Richard went through a destructive period in his life. He was rarely sober; he ended up screwing three girls in two days, never knowing what their names were. He almost lost his job when he shoved a photographer out of his way, but ended up with a suspension for a few weeks considering the circumstances. All in all, he was slowly killing himself because he didn't care anymore and it was worse than last time.

    The thing is and this was the really scary part, he kept telling everybody that he was okay. He had convinced himself that despite a few minor mishaps, as he liked to call them, he was okay. When he didn't show up to meet Jack for breakfast for their usual weekly morning outing that's when Jack got concerned because in 12 years he had never not showed up. Later that evening Jack and Sara went to find Richard when he wouldn't answer his phone. Mike and Nicole would check the hospitals and police stations just as precaution. They finally found him at his own apartment not answering the door.

He still wouldn't let them in and Jack ended up breaking the door just to get inside. They found him in the kitchen sitting on the floor with a half empty bottle of scotch just staring at a picture of Paula. It looked like he had been there for days. He was a mess and he looked like he had not taken care of himself in days. Sara prepared some coffee and Jack took the bottle of scotch away while Richard ignored him, trying to act like Jack wasn't really there.

Jack looked at his brother and said in a sarcastic tone "If you're going to kill yourself, you're still not doing right. Shooting yourself would be good and you don't even have to clean up the mess."

Richard looked at him with half-cocked smile, but he didn't say anything. He didn't want to, but it was a good sign that he looked up at his brother. Jack sat down next to Richard and said. "I understand what you've lost and if you're going to wait until it doesn't hurt anymore then I'll stay with you."

After a few minutes, Richard finally spoke and he said. "How can you know what's I've lost, the woman you love is standing there making coffee."

"Glad to hear you speaking again. Maybe I don't know the full weight of what you're going through, but I know what it means to lose something."

Richard looked away and replied. "Yeah, but you got her back. I'll never get mine back. I wish I'd never loved her."

"Don't say that, loving her made you a better person, you can't deny that."

Richard didn't respond to that, he continues to look away. Jack continued by saying, "I wish I had answers for you, but all I have are more questions."

"There are no answers," Richard said. "There never was."

"I guess if there are answers then all they bring are more questions. Maybe all we can do is learn to live with those questions and try to make some kind of sense out of them."

"How do you make sense out of death...out of a death that shouldn't be, because she shouldn't have died, not after getting her life back in order."

Jack looked at his brother instead of a wall and said. "I don't know, but I think we have to try -it's the only way we can know anything about tragic deaths that seem meaningless."

"What's the use, I seem to get more sense out of that damn bottle of scotch. Speaking of..." Richard tried to get up and grab the bottle, but Jack stopped him and Sara handed him a cup coffee saying to him that he needed to drink that instead. Richard did drink some of the coffee.

Jack said to his brother. "I don't know what to tell you in order to get beyond this tragedy, but we're here for you."

Richard said. "I don't think there is anything to say. Paula's gone and I loved her. She was taken from me after we both found our way again. The only thing I can do is blame God who has a very sadistic sense of humor."

It was hard for Jack to respond to that, but he asked Richard one question. "Richard was it worth knowing her, worth loving her?"

Richard looked at him and said without a doubt, "Yes it was."

"You see you wouldn't trade that for anything no matter unfair it is for someone like her die so tragically. Maybe Trinidad was right, accidents happen all the time and all that matters is how we act upon them."

"Are you trying to get me off this floor," Richard asked.

"Actually I don't care if you get off the floor as long as you don't forget to breath-living is the only thing I want you to do because if you haven't noticed I kind of need my brother."

Richard laughed, which he hadn't done it a while. He said. "Of course you do, you wouldn't have a wild side if it weren't for me.

Jack got up and pulled Richard off the floor. He said to his brother, "I know you have to go through whatever this is alone in order to grieve, but we're all here for you. She did change your life and if she hadn't come along when she did, there's no telling what kind of person you would be now. If nothing else take comfort in that."

Richard hugged his brother and said, "Thank You, I can't stop missing her."

"I know-we all do- but remember her for who she was and how she made you feel. Do that and she will always be with you."

They hugged again and Sara walked over and hugged them both. Richard shed a few tears, he actually cried quite a bit. Mike and Nicole showed up not too long after that and they all drank coffee and told their stories of Paula and how she and Richard first met in college and then later in Life. They were amusing stories and they made everybody feel better about her tragic death.

Sometimes that's how life can be, tragic and unfair, and death is just as natural as a happy ending. It's not meant to always be understood, but the grieving in no small way helps us to be better people and to be more human in a world where our humanity sometimes escapes us. It would be nice to say that there is always a happy ending, but it's hardly ever the case. Death makes us stronger and tragedy is just as important when it comes to living a great life as strange as it sound.

Paula's funeral was nice and it was special in its own way as friends and family remembered her for who she was and what she had become. Her journey in life was beautiful-tragic and poetic, but true and beautiful. There were no final thoughts for Richard in a letter or for her friends, but what she meant to them was enough. She changed all of their lives in some way and that was enough; actually, it was perfect.

Although death is a part of this story, it's not the end. Like all great stories, it ends with a choice. In the sex game, the only way to succeed is to make a choice, to live with that choice, and to finally, become that choice. It may not make much sense, but we are the choices we make. Our lives are all about choices, nothing more to say.

A month later Jen went in to labor. It was a long labor so everybody happened to be at the hospital for about 36 hours. Nicole and Ashley who both worked at the same hospital happened to be working so everybody was called when Jen arrived. They all pretty much camped out in the waiting area and Nicole and Ashley never really went home except to change into new scrubs. They weren't going to miss this either for they were part of the family. Jen and Jarrod welcomed a baby boy and it was certainly time to celebrate again. The most important choice they made resulted in a new life being brought into the world.

The female doctor who happened to be on call when their regular doctor was away did a great job and she was welcomed by everybody. She was a surprise because nobody knew her and Jen and Jarrod were unsure of what she could do, but like a great accident, she did an outstanding job. Also, by accident, she bumped into Richard and throughout the course of 36 hours they talked a little bit and got to know each other. They even made each other laugh a couple times. Nicole was the first one to take notice of this and she said to Richard. "You know she's single, you should ask her out."

    Richard scoffed at the notion; he still thought that he wasn't ready yet. But after awhile everybody got on his case and said the same thing. While everybody was noticing the new baby, Richard kept noticing the doctor. He thought about it for a moment and made a hard choice, it was time to get up off the floor, breath in and out again, take a new step, and take that chance. If accidents happen all the time then all we can do is act upon them, and in the end, hopefully it will be a good thing. However, it never will unless we do take that chance, that's the catch 22 of the whole thing. For that's the sex game; it's up and down, back and forth, until we've come full circle.

    Richard walked up to the doctor and said. " I never introduced myself earlier. I'm Richard, it's nice to meet you."

    "I'm Doctor Keaton."

"I know. I was wondering if you would like to get a cup of coffee sometime."

She gave Richard a surprised look and then responded. "Thank you, but no, I don't go on dates with people I meet at the hospital."

"I'm not asking you on a date-that might come later, if we like each other."

She laughed and then replied. "I don't date at all; with all the bad men I've dated I just can't do it anymore."

"I don't really date either, but I just wanted to buy you a cup of coffee. I've enjoyed talking with you and I would like to do it some more."

"It's flattering, but really I can't."

"It's just coffee, it doesn't have to be anything else."

"I just don't want to go through something bad again and chances are it would be bad. I know we met by accident, but that's probably a bad thing." Dr. Keaton started to walk off after saying that but she turned back around to look at Richard

Richard said as she turned around. "Accidents happen all the time- all that matters is how we act when they happen. What do you have to lose by having a cup of coffee with me. You know it could be bad for the both of us, but how will you ever know for sure? It could also be a good thing."

She stopped and turned around, stared at him for a moment and then smiled at him. She said to Richard. "Alright then, meet me across the street in 20 minutes."

Richard smiled at her while she just stared at him waiting for him to say something. She was attracted to him, but she wasn't going to let her guard down with him, at least not yet.

Richard while still smiling asked her. "Do you have a first name?"

Still smiling she replied. "It's Brandy."

"A human being is part of a whole, called by us the Universe, a part limited in time and space. He experiences himself, his thoughts and feelings, as something separated from the rest--a kind of optical delusion of his consciousness. This delusion is a kind of prison for us, restricting us to our personal desires and to affection for a few persons nearest us. Our task must be to free ourselves from this prison by widening our circles of compassion to embrace all living creatures and the whole of nature in its beauty."

∞∞∞∞∞

"From the standpoint of daily life, however, there is one thing we do know: that we are here for the sake of each other - above all for those upon whose smile and well-being our own happiness depends, and also for the countless unknown souls with whose fate we are connected by a bond of sympathy. Many times a day I realize how much my own outer and inner life is built upon the labors of my fellow men, both living and dead, and how earnestly I must exert myself in order to give in return as much as I have received."

~ Albert Einstein

What do I know of love, not much? Of course, I've been in love before and even had my heart broken once, but I'm far from an expert when it comes to love. Is there really an expert on love, maybe not? For me the only certainty I have is that we never know who we truly are unless we choose to see the truth that stares us in the mirror. Or it's when we cannot hide behind the mask that we often put on and usually ignore.

~ Marcus Blake

Printed in the United States
126123LV00001B/32/P